RAGS TO WITCHES

A WESTWICK WITCHES COZY MYSTERY

COLLEEN CROSS

SLICE PUBLISHING

Rags to Witches: A Westwick Witches Cozy Mystery

Categories: cozy mysteries, witches wizards, paranormal cozy humorous mystery, cosy mystery, funny mysteries, female lead sleuth women amateur sleuths private investigators, cozy mystery books, suspense thrillers and mysteries best sellers, female detectives

eBook ISBN: 978-1-988272-13-9

Published by Slice Publishing

ISBN: 978-1-988272-12-12

WIN, LOSE, OR DRAW...

Cendrine West can't catch a break. She's close to landing a new job, and things are getting cozy with sexy sheriff Tyler Gates. All that changes when she is kidnapped by renegade witch Aunt Pearl, who is hell bent on avenging a friend's untimely death. Its Las Vegas or bust...for all the wrong reasons.

Rocco Racatelli is a hunky Vegas kingpin—and the next mob target. Lady Luck has dealt him a losing hand and he wants revenge. When Aunt Pearl is a little too eager to help, project Vegas Vendetta quickly escalates into an all-out mob turf war. As the witches are thrust into Sin City's seamy underworld, bodies pile up and secrets are exposed.

It's not just the Las Vegas heat that's scorching...Rocco is intent on winning Cen's heart. But she only wants the man she left behind in Westwick Corners. All she has to do is solve a murder, out-magic her ornery aunt, and take down the Las Vegas mafia. What could possibly go wrong?

When organized crime meets unorganized magic, anything can happen! As the body count climbs, it's clear that Cen needs more than a miracle in the desert to set things right.

LISTEN IN AUDIO!

I needed a job. I needed gas, and I needed a break.

The odds of getting any of those were stacked against me. My gas tank was empty and the Westwick Corners Gas N' Go's solitary gas pump was broken. The ancient pump had no intercom, and I abhorred the thought of walking all the way to the cashier in my three-inch heels.

I was already running late for my job interview at *The Shady Creek Tattler*. It was humiliating to admit that my own newspaper, *The Westwick Corners Weekly*, was just days from bankruptcy. The last thing I wanted was to work for the competition, but I needed money. I was conflicted. I didn't want to turn my back on Westwick Corners, the almost-ghost town we were trying to revitalize. But I needed to earn a living.

All of the decent jobs were an hour away in Shady Creek. I had realized too late that Westwick Corners was too small to support much of anything, including the newspaper I had bought from the retiring owner last year. *The Westwick Corners Weekly* had been an impulse purchase. My plan to buy myself a dream job had become a never-ending money pit.

My last hope of remaining solvent was the part-time reporter job in Shady Creek. At least I could eke out a living while I got my newspaper back on track. But even that was in jeopardy if I couldn't fill my gas tank. I waved my hands frantically towards the reflective glass windows, hoping the cashier inside would see me and get the gas pump going again.

Nothing.

I swore under my breath as I scanned the asphalt. My spirits lifted when I spotted a skinny freckle-faced man-boy standing beside a gigantic RV. The gas station attendant looked about fifteen going on twenty, and wore a too-big Gas N' Go shirt and baggy shorts. I hadn't seen him around town before, so I guessed he was a recent arrival. Which was weird in itself, since we rarely had visitors, let alone new residents. Gossip usually preceded any new residents by at least a few days.

I waved the attendant over, but he ignored me as he checked the air on the RV tires. That wasn't a surprise. Anyone moving to West-wick Corners was usually running away from someone or someplace. Almost-ghost towns weren't exactly high on the list of top places to live, but they made perfect hiding places. Nobody ever came looking.

My hopes soared when the RV door opened and Aunt Pearl stepped out. She waved frantically and practically flew towards me. Few seventy-year-old women moved as fast, but Mom's oldest sister had a secret advantage. Like the rest of us West women, she was a witch.

"I won, I won!" My ninety-pound aunt screeched to a stop on the concrete island and teetered before losing her balance and falling against me.

"Watch out!" The gas nozzle flew from my hand as I jumped back to avoid her. The nozzle bounced off the side of my rusty and dented Honda. And, suddenly, it worked.

Gas spewed on the cracked asphalt like a Texas gusher. I had one of those automatic gadgets that attached to the nozzle and had locked it in the "on" position. Just my luck that the nozzle had unjammed at the exact moment it fell from my hand.

More money down the drain.

I scrambled to grab the gas nozzle as it spiraled out of control from the pressure of the spraying gas. All I succeeded in capturing was fuel. It sprayed all over my brand new dress and blazer that I had bought especially for my job interview.

I winced as the spray stung my freshly shaven legs. Gas accumulated in puddles at my feet. I stood in shock, soaking wet, furious, and at a loss for words.

That got the attendant's attention, and he hurried towards us. "Hey, you gotta pay for that!"

The nozzle bucked from the fuel pressure and gyrated wildly. I finally grabbed the nozzle, but before I could turn it away from me it drenched me again from head to toe. The only saving grace was that I still wore my sunglasses.

Gas sprayed up my nostrils and covered my sunglasses. I dropped the nozzle as my hands flew to my face to block the spray. I wiped my finger across the sunglass lenses, but everything, including Aunt Pearl, was blurred.

"Don't hurt me!" Aunt Pearl screamed as she stepped backwards and waved her arms in the air.

"Grab the nozzle, quick. Help me, I can't see!" My arms flailed as I groped blindly for the nozzle. My right hand finally closed around the nozzle, but when I tried to pry my gas gadget from the pump handle, my fingernail bent backwards.

"Ouch!" I dropped the nozzle and it sprayed my ankles as it fell to the pavement. I groped for the handle, but couldn't get a grip strong enough to hold on. My fingers grew numb at my fruitless attempts.

I flailed my arms, trying to grab the handle with my limited vision. That set me off balance and I tripped and fell off the concrete island.

After what seemed like an eternity, the pump suddenly stopped. I ripped off my sunglasses and wiped fuel from my forehead with the back of my hand.

The attendant stood by the gas pump, nozzle in one hand and my nozzle lock gadget in the other. "Don't touch anything. I'll pump it for you."

I mumbled thanks as I rose to my feet, soaking wet. I shivered, despite the late summer heat.

"That's a lotta gas. Five gallons gone to waste." Aunt Pearl snapped her fingers. "Just like that."

Aunt Pearl was somewhat of a pyromaniac, so wasted gas bordered on travesty.

"You could have helped me." I slowly shook my head as I looked down at my ruined dress. Words couldn't describe the despair I felt right now. Everything I did seemed to take me one step closer to financial ruin.

"You need to help yourself, Cen. You've got what it takes, if only you applied yourself. One way or another, you'll come to terms with your supernatural talents." Aunt Pearl patted my back. "You have a choice."

"I am not cheating." I turned to the attendant, but he had retreated to the RV, out of earshot. "I don't want any unfair advantages, that's all."

"Witchcraft isn't cheating if you're a witch. Stop pretending you're someone you're not."

I was already in a bad mood. The last thing I needed was an argument with my ornery aunt. "I just want to be like everyone else."

"Well, you aren't, so you better get used to it." Aunt Pearl snorted. "Why are you wasting time with a day job? Anyone else with your talents would be making good use of them. Instead, you just let them go to waste."

"I want to earn an honest living." The words came out before I could stop them.

"Being a witch is somehow dishonest?" Aunt Pearl's anger cut through her words.

It irked her that I hadn't kept up my magic lessons at Pearl's Charm School. I always meant to, but other things seemed to get in the way. And it didn't feel right, using special talents that regular people lacked. I hadn't done anything to earn them. I just had the good fortune to be born into the West family of witches.

"I'm late for my interview. Can't you just reverse everything and put some gas in my car?" Aunt Pearl was an extremely talented witch. It would be effortless for her.

"I could. But why should I?"

"Aunt Pearl, please. I'll make it up to you." I needed this job.

She shook her head. "You kids today have such a sense of entitlement. Nothing worthwhile is ever easy, Cen."

"But it's so easy," I protested. "For you."

"It could be for you too. Practice makes perfect, Cendrine. All you have to do is apply yourself. Why is that so hard?"

The gas station attendant finished pumping my gas and held his hand out for payment. I glanced at the meter and reached inside my passenger window and grabbed my wallet out of my purse on the front passenger seat. I fished my last twenty-dollar bill out and tossed my wallet back into the car. I handed him the money, annoyed that most of the fuel I had just paid for was in a puddle on the payment. Hardly any fuel had actually made it into my gas tank.

"Uh, Cen, this is Wilt Chamberlain."

I nodded at the skinny man-boy, who was freckled, white, and looked nothing like the famous basketball player from years ago. He was older than I had originally guessed: probably in his early twenties. His skin was so pale it was almost bluish, save for a diamond-shaped birthmark on his forehead. It was the color of rust and sat dead center on his forehead, like a target.

"Next time, ask for help." Wilt replaced the gas nozzle in the holder. "Now I got to close down the pump and clean this mess up."

"There's no time for cleaning," Aunt Pearl waved at the RV. "We've got to get on the road."

"Huh?" I frowned, wondering what my aunt was up to now.

Aunt Pearl waved her hand. "Forget the interview, Cen. I have a job for you."

I shook my head. "I am not working at Pearl's Charm School."

She smiled brightly. "That's not what I had in mind. I have a mission for you. It's undercover."

I shook my head. "Not interested."

We watched Wilt walk back inside the station. He pulled out a giant key ring and locked up the station door.

"Hey! You haven't given me my change yet!" I glanced at the gas pump. According to the pump, my total gas bill was less than ten dollars, and that included all the gas I had spilled. Whatever had ended up in my tank wasn't enough to even leave town, let alone make it to Shady Creek.

"Wilt!"

He purposely ignored me.

I grabbed the gas nozzle and waved it in the air like a weapon.

He didn't bite. "Sorry, we're closed."

I placed the nozzle in my gas tank. I switched the pump on, this time without the accessory. It was no use. Either Wilt had shut off the pump or it really was out of gas.

I swore under my breath as I turned to a smirking Aunt Pearl. "Why won't you help me?" My eyes locked on the red gas can she held in one hand.

"Forget about the gas. I won the lottery, Cen. I'm rich. I can afford just about anything. Including unlimited gas." She swung her gas can back and forth in an arc.

I nodded towards the RV. "You'll need it with that tank. Where did you get it?"

Aunt Pearl seemed almost giddy, which I supposed would be what any lottery winner would feel like. Except I doubted her story. My aunt liked to get attention, and I just assumed the lottery story was a giant lie, supplemented with white magic props like the shiny RV and even the gas.

The gas.

Aunt Pearl's five-gallon gas can made a sloshing noise, which meant it contained gas. Five gallons would get me to Shady Creek and my job interview. Problem solved.

"Aunt Pearl! Is that a full can of gas? I need a favor."

"You're a witch, Cendrine. Make your own gas."

"Not now, Aunt Pearl." It was Aunt Pearl's version of tough love. It bothered her to no end that I neglected my witchcraft lessons.

"Oh, I forgot. You don't know how." Aunt Pearl stuck out her lower lip in a fake pout.

I wanted nothing more than to prove her wrong. But I wasn't even good at that. All I had to show for myself was a failed business, loose change, and bad luck. Everything I did seemed to backfire. My life truly sucked, and I had no idea how to make it better.

CHAPTER 2

I glared at Aunt Pearl. Just because the West family's supernatural talents were a poorly kept secret around Westwick Corners didn't mean we had to flaunt them. For generations, we had operated under a "don't ask, don't tell" policy. Given Wilt was new in town, he probably had no idea about our witchcraft. Until Aunt Pearl, of course.

"Stop worrying about trivial things and hop aboard. I'll drive you to your job interview." Aunt Pearl gave me a sickly sweet smile that I knew was fake.

Wilt frowned, obviously disappointed at the idea of me coming along for the ride.

I was afraid to ask. I did anyway. "Why do you need an RV?" I also wanted to ask my aunt why she needed Wilt to accompany her, but it seemed rude for me to ask with him standing right there.

Aunt Pearl rolled her eyes. "I don't need it, Cen. I want it. It's my very own hotel on wheels. Pearl's Palace, I call it."

She had obviously conjured it up, but I couldn't confront her in front of the gas station attendant. The fact that the West family were witches wasn't exactly a well-kept secret in Westwick Corners.

Since Aunt Pearl was forever showing off her magic, I wondered how much this guy had seen. The brand new thirty-foot RV didn't exactly blend in, and it probably cost more than I made in a couple of years. If it was real, which of course it wasn't. Just like Cinderella's coach, it would vanish in a poof after a certain amount of time. Which, if you were a passenger, made it a ticking time bomb of sorts.

"I'll drive you," she said. "Shady Creek is on the way to Vegas. It's no trouble."

Against my better judgment, I agreed.

Aunt Pearl opened the RV door and motioned me inside. "Hop in. I've got another passenger to pick up, and then we'll head to Shady Creek and drop you off."

I couldn't imagine anyone who wanted to go on a Las Vegas vacation with Aunt Pearl. None of her handful of friends lived nearby. It was none of my concern, I told myself. Some things I was better off not knowing.

I settled in at the kitchen nook and spread out my wet dress to help it dry faster. I found it odd that my aunt hadn't pushed her usual agenda of using my own magic to get to the interview. She had criticized my lack of practice but was still quick to offer me a ride.

Aunt Pearl climbed up into the passenger seat and turned around in her seat. She motioned to the driver's seat, occupied by the skinny gas station attendant. "I hired Wilt as my driver."

I had forgotten that Aunt Pearl didn't drive. "What about your friend?"

She dismissed me with a wave. "It's a long drive in something this big. Besides, I'm rich. I can afford a chauffeur."

Still, it seemed bizarre that Wilt was along for the ride. It was better not to make a big deal out of things with Aunt Pearl because she was easily riled.

I turned my thoughts back to my interview. I needed to

somehow get back from Shady Creek, but I'd worry about that later.

There's nothing worse than a witch down on her luck. Except maybe a witch who got a little too lucky. Put the two of them together and anything could happen.

CHAPTER 3

"*B*uckle up." Aunt Pearl fastened her seat belt and hollered. "Vegas baby, or bust!"

We lurched forward and peeled out of the gas station parking lot. "Whoa. I never said—"

My aunt turned around in her seat. "Relax, Cen. We'll get you to your job interview."

I gripped the kitchenette table as Wilt made a sharp turn onto Main Street. Maybe I had a death wish or something. I couldn't think of any other reason for riding with a maniac driver and an ornery witch sidekick.

"We're headed in the wrong direction!" Wilt and Aunt Pearl either ignored me or didn't hear. Aside from the fact we weren't headed to Shady Creek, Wilt's driving was making me fear for my life.

Yet here I was, seemingly powerless to help myself. Wilt reached the edge of town and headed up the winding road to The Westwick Corners Inn.

"Why are we going home?" My family's mansion had been converted to a boutique bed and breakfast that we operated mostly on the weekends. We also lived on the property, so now I was back where I started. Except without a car this time.

Reaching my interview on time seemed less likely by the minute. I reached beside me for my purse, only to realize that I had left it on the passenger seat of my car.

Mom waved as our RV pulled into the circular driveway. She climbed into the RV and dragged a large suitcase to the RV's rear bed. She returned seconds later, gasping for breath. Then she collapsed in a heap on the opposite side of the kitchenette nook. "That was heavy."

"Mom? What's going on? You can't leave the Inn. We've got guests coming." The Inn couldn't function without Mom. She was chef, manager, and front desk clerk, all rolled into one. Aunt Pearl was officially the chief housekeeper, but she was completely unreliable. I usually played backup to Aunt Pearl, since she set her own unpredictable hours and pretty much answered to no one. She was a witch first, with her job at the Inn a distant second.

I, on the other hand, seemed to be juggling a couple of jobs with little money to show for it. Working for myself or my family just wasn't keeping me afloat financially or otherwise. If I wanted a future, I had to reconsider my options. *The Shady Creek Tattler* wasn't exactly corporate America, but it was at least a step up from anything in tiny Westwick Corners.

Aunt Pearl interrupted. "We've got urgent family business to take care of, Cen. We haven't got all day, so stop all the questions and let Ruby catch her breath."

"What are you talking about? The Inn is our family business."

"I'll explain later." Aunt Pearl waved her arms impatiently. "We've got to get moving before it's too late."

"Explain now." I crossed my arms.

"Sorry, but our mission is top secret. Everything's on a need to know basis, and right now you don't need to know anything. I'll tell you when the time is right." Aunt Pearl glanced at her watch, then turned towards the driver's seat. "We're behind schedule. Floor it, Wilt."

The G-force slammed me back in my seat as the RV accelerated.

"Everything's fine, Cen." Mom glanced uncertainly at Aunt Pearl. "We don't have any guests until Friday and I'm bored. I could use a road trip."

I frowned. Mom was a horrible liar. Aunt Pearl had obviously put her up to this. Whatever it was had to be pretty serious for Mom to abandon the Inn and leave town.

"Huh?" Mom's big suitcase made me all the more suspicious about the supposedly impromptu road trip. She had found time to pack, so the trip must have been preplanned.

Mom ignored me. Instead she braced herself against the Arborite table as the RV hurtled down the steep hill that led off our property to the main road out of town.

Mom seemed stressed, though she tried not to show it. "It's nice to sit down. This RV is bigger than I thought."

"Where did you get the RV, Aunt Pearl?" Everyone seemed to be in on her scheme but me.

No answer.

"Aunt Pearl?"

My aunt turned around and grimaced as she squeezed her nose with her thumb and index finger. "Geesh, Cendrine, you stink to high heaven."

"Don't change the subject. It's the gas. You were going to help me clean up, remember?"

Aunt Pearl ignored me and opened the front passenger window.

Mom nodded in agreement. She sat across from me in the kitchen nook. "No one's going to hire you smelling like gas. It's just as well you have to reschedule your interview."

"I am not rescheduling." I opened the window, hoping the breeze would dissipate the gas fumes. Timing was tight, but I still had a chance of making the interview. All I had to do was remain silent and cooperative until I got dropped off in Shady Creek.

I glanced around the RV and noticed a half-full bottle of water lying in the sink. I rose to grab it and teetered on my heels as the RV barreled down the hill. The RV screeched to a halt at the stop sign at the bottom of our driveway.

Just as quickly Wilt stepped on the gas and tore around the corner. I recovered my balance and grabbed the water bottle. I had barely scrambled back to my seat when the RV skidded across to the wrong side of the road before swinging back on track. I unscrewed the cap and dabbed a small amount of water onto the front of my dress.

Mom raised her brows. "It's a bit early for that, don't you think?"

I frowned, puzzled by her comment until I recognized the odor. The bottle contained vodka, not water.

Now I reeked of alcohol. I would never make it past security, let alone to Human Resources. I'd violate the drug and alcohol policy before I even got past the screening interview.

I swore under my breath and turned to Mom. "I can't go to the interview like this. Can you give me some special help?" That was our code word for magic. I braced myself for a lecture on neglecting my witchcraft lessons. Mom was usually more forgiving than Aunt Pearl, though both constantly criticized my lack of discipline. I had to admit I had different priorities. They were right about one thing, though. I couldn't cast a spell if my life depended on it.

"I don't understand why you feel the need to leave Westwick Corners." Mom shook her head, disappointed. "You've got full-time work at the Inn if you want it. You don't need a reporter job in another town. Journalism isn't your calling, Cen, and I don't understand why you're so ashamed of your heritage. You could have pretty much anything if you just practiced your witchcraft."

I remained silent. I couldn't explain to two expert witches that I wanted the one thing witchcraft couldn't give me—to fit in and just be a normal twenty-something woman, with a regular job and a normal family. I craved acceptance, something you simply couldn't cast with a spell. I wanted to be like everyone else. "I just want to live my own life. Magic causes more trouble than it's worth sometimes."

"You've got so much natural talent, Cen." Mom sighed. "You're squandering your abilities. One day you'll wake up and realize everything too late. I just don't want you to regret it."

My shoulders sagged. Even Mom was on Aunt Pearl's side. I was stuck. "Aunt Pearl didn't really win the lottery, did she?" I was sure it was one of my aunt's white lies. "She conjured it up."

Mom shook her head. "It's real, Cen. Wilt even sold her the winning ticket at the gas station. That's one reason she hired him as driver."

As if on cue Aunt Pearl turned in her seat. "He's my lucky charm."

I jolted back in my seat as Wilt punched the gas pedal. "The lottery was last night. She hasn't had time to cash the ticket, let alone shop for an RV."

"You know Pearl. She works fast."

Exactly what I was afraid of. Aunt Pearl could wreak havoc in a matter of minutes. I slid sideways on the bench seat and stomped my foot down to stop myself from falling into the aisle.

The RV shuddered as it gained speed and fought the wind. I was crazy-scared, since we hadn't even left the highway on-ramp yet.

"Slow down!" My knuckles turned white as I gripped the Arborite table.

Wilt ignored my pleas and we careened onto the highway.

Within minutes a police siren blared behind us. The flashing lights reflected in the rear view mirror as Wilt lurched to a stop on the side of the road. I jolted back in my seat, relieved that we had been pulled over. The traffic stop had probably saved us from carnage on the Interstate.

Mom's face turned ghostly white. She cracked open the window and leaned out. She looked as though she might be sick.

I turned around to say something to Wilt, but he was too busy cursing and rolling down his window to pay me any attention.

I craned my neck to see the sheriff's SUV parked behind the RV, angled out police-style.

Great.

Sheriff Tyler Gates was the last person I wanted to see right now. Not because I didn't like him. In fact, I liked him a lot. Too much, in fact. I had broken off my wedding to another man because of him, only he didn't know that. I wasn't about to admit it, but it was the truth.

"He's at it again. I'm being persecuted." Aunt Pearl didn't like the sheriff one bit. I had no doubt that my law-breaking aunt was about to embarrass us all.

Tyler and I had been secretly dating for the last few months, meeting in Shady Creek to avoid both gossip and interference from Aunt Pearl. She had successfully run every other sheriff out of town, and losing Tyler was a risk I wasn't willing to take.

I slouched down in my seat, hoping Tyler wouldn't notice me as he walked by the RV window.

He immediately spotted me and smiled. I smiled back, and Mom gave a quick wave.

Aunt Pearl muttered something from the front passenger seat.

"Hello, Pearl." Tyler peered in through the driver's side window. He seemed to hold his own against my ornery aunt.

Aunt Pearl grunted something under her breath. I suspected she had more up her sleeve than a conjured-up lottery win and a magical RV.

I held my breath, hoping she wouldn't start an argument.

Tyler's gaze shifted to Mom and me. He nodded and smiled. For a split second I considered asking Tyler for a ride to Shady Creek, but just as quickly dismissed it. Aside from angering Aunt Pearl, it might reveal our secret relationship.

"License and registration please." Tyler Gates peered inside as he waited for the documents. "Going on vacation?"

"We're heading to Vegas," Pearl said. "That against the law?"

Tyler frowned as his eyes locked on mine.

I shook my head. Nobody was going to Vegas, least of all me. Even if I missed my interview, I'd still make our date. Tyler and I were having dinner at a fancy new French restaurant in Shady Creek, far from prying eyes of friends and family. Until then, I didn't want him to get close enough to see or smell my ruined dress. I'd shop for another dress right after my interview.

A trace of a smile played on Tyler's lips as he turned to Aunt Pearl. "No, but a broken taillight is. You'll have to get that fixed."

"We're heading to the shop right now, Officer," Wilt said. "The part we need is in Shady Creek."

I relaxed at the mention of Shady Creek. Lately my timing always seemed a little off, just like it was for this interview. It was like fate had intervened or something. Maybe that was a good thing, since I'd rather not work at the *Shady Creek Tattler*. But I still needed to earn a living.

I slid closer to the window to air out my eau du gasoline smell. My clothes had dried quickly in the summer heat. Other than the faint odor, there were no visible stains from the gasoline fiasco. Maybe things would work out after all.

The sheriff let us off with a warning and Wilt promised to get the taillight fixed pronto.

I refocused on the highway as we passed the highway sign informing us that we had reached the Shady Creek city limits. I felt a glimmer of hope as I checked my watch. We hadn't been stopped as long as I thought. There was a small chance I might make my interview after all, thanks to Wilt's excessive speed. Which, from Mom's panicked expression, was freaking her out.

It seemed odd that Mom was even on the trip since she hated any kind of traveling. She rarely even went to Shady Creek. Las Vegas might as well have been on another planet. Mom probably came along only because Aunt Pearl could find herself in a whole mess of trouble in Las Vegas.

Suddenly the RV rocked and careened across the center line. The forest along the highway became a blur of green, brown and asphalt.

I jerked my head around as we sped down the highway and passed the Shady Creek turnoff. "We just missed my exit."

Wilt turned around in his seat and the RV swerved into the oncoming lane.

"Watch the road!" Mom's knuckles turned white as she clenched the Arborite table. "You're going to get us killed!"

I screamed as I fell off the bench seat and into the aisle, sure we were about to die in a head-on collision. I rolled on the floor a few feet before I slammed into the kitchen cupboards.

Just as suddenly the RV reversed course and returned to the lane. I rose to my feet just in time to see us narrowly miss a semi-trailer coming in the opposite direction. We were on the wrong side of a four-lane highway. Wilt was even less qualified as a driver than as a gas station attendant. The trip was quickly headed for disaster.

I returned to my seat at the kitchen nook, breathless. I looked for my cell phone but came up empty. I swore when I realized that both my phone and the *Shady Creek Tattler's* phone number were still in my purse on my car seat. It was now five minutes after my interview time and we were headed in the opposite direction.

I had blown my chance. The newspaper wasn't likely to hire a reporter who blew off interviews and didn't even have the courtesy to call.

I couldn't even call Tyler. I might even be a no-show for our date. What would he think of me?

Aunt Pearl turned around in her seat. "Cen, stop all your fussing.

You don't need that job. In fact, you never have to work another day in your life. I've got you covered. I won the lottery, remember?"

"How much did you win, exactly?"

My aunt dismissed me with a wave of her hand. "All you need to know is that I pay top dollar. You'll have to pass probation, of course."

I sighed. Another excuse for Aunt Pearl to order me around. The lottery win was just another of her tales. I didn't believe her outrageous story for a minute, and the last person I wanted to be beholden to was my wacky aunt. "Why the RV? You know WICCA rules prohibit magic just for the sake of it."

WICCA, or the *Witches International Community Craft Association*, had strict rules about the frivolous use of magic. Every spell needed a purpose, and flaunting magic indiscriminately was subject to a hefty fine. Aunt Pearl flaunted the rules with reckless abandon and always got away with it.

It was also against the rules to talk openly about witchcraft, but by this point I was so fed up. I really didn't care if Wilt heard me or not.

"I am not breaking any rules," Aunt Pearl snapped. "If you practiced your craft more, you'd know there are loopholes."

"Let's not fight." Mom turned to me. "You're awfully testy, Cen. You really do need this vacation."

Aunt Pearl had apparently bewitched my neurotic Mom and turned her into a laid-back zombie. We were all being kidnapped, whether we knew it or not. All I took comfort from was that at least the RV wasn't stolen. Sheriff Tyler Gates would have checked the plates when he pulled us over.

We passed the next exit sign in a flash and I got the sense there was no turning back. I turned to Mom. "You're letting her kidnap me?" Aside from missing the exit, we were gaining speed at an alarming rate. My pulse quickened as the RV once again shuddered against the wind force. I tightened my seat belt.

"Now Cen, you know Pearl doesn't intentionally break laws." Mom's words were completely at odds with her body language. The color drained from her face as she gripped the table edge. Mom was holding something back. "Only when absolutely necessary."

"It's never necessary," I protested. Aunt Pearl tended to act first and think later. I just wished she were more law-abiding and less of a troublemaker. But she'd already had plenty of run-ins with Sheriff Tyler Gates, and law enforcement outside Westwick Corners wasn't nearly as forgiving.

"I don't care what the reason is. Turn this thing around and take me back."

"Not a chance, missy." Aunt Pearl let out a whoop and waved her boney fist in the air. "Whoo-hoo! Vegas baby, here we come!"

"Let me out and I'll hitchhike back."

"You are not hitchhiking." Mom wagged her finger. "You know how dangerous that is? I can't let you do that."

"No." Aunt Pearl rose from the passenger seat and joined us at the kitchen table. "You have to come with us and celebrate."

"I don't understand. If you really won millions in the lottery, why gamble and risk losing it?" I never understood why lottery winners kept playing. I'd quit gambling and just be happy with my good fortune. I'm not very lucky though, so the odds of that happening were slim.

"It's an adrenaline rush." Mom nodded towards Aunt Pearl. "She can't help it."

I glanced at Wilt in the driver's seat, who for once was focused on the road and not our conversation. "You're a witch, for crying out loud. You can conjure up pretty much anything else with a spell."

"This Vegas-mobile isn't magic, Cen. It's a test drive from Shady Creek Motors."

"I doubt they expected you to take it on a seventeen-hour road trip."

Aunt Pearl shrugged. "They told me to keep it as long as I wanted. I'm feeling lucky and I want to go to Sin City."

"Gambling never pays off."

"Maybe not for you, Cen," Aunt Pearl said. "Why are you such a negative Nelly?"

"I'm just being practical about the—"

Aunt Pearl rolled her eyes. "Okay, so we're celebrating my lottery win, but that's not the real reason we're going."

"It's a celebration of life," Mom added.

"Someone died? Who? We don't know anyone in Vegas."

Aunt Pearl ignored my question. "We'll go to the funeral, maybe take in a couple of shows and do some shopping. A girls' night out."

"It will take us all night to get there. Vegas is eighteen hours away."

"Plans need to change sometimes," Aunt Pearl said. "You're so inflexible it's ridiculous."

"But I already made plans. You can't just change them without consulting me." I was encased in a steel and fiberglass prison, hurtling down the highway with no way out.

"Sorry, Cen, but you're needed at the funeral." Mom patted my hand. "This is one celebration you can't afford to miss."

CHAPTER 4

I had a pounding headache from the gas and alcohol fumes that still wafted up from my dress. While the dress had dried, the smell had somehow grown more concentrated. It seemed to permeate every nook and cranny of the RV with each passing mile. Probably because Aunt Pearl refused to turn on the A/C and had cranked up the heat instead.

I wiped sweat from my forehead as I tried to make sense of the mystery funeral and the strange turn of events. "Who died and what have I got to do with it?"

"We'll explain everything sooner or later. But right now we've got a job to do." Mom studied me with soulful eyes. "We need your help, Cen. Remember Mrs. Racatelli?"

"The Mafia wife?"

"Don't call her that. Carla had a life of her own. Besides, there's no proof linking Tommy to the mob. He just traveled a lot and kept odd hours."

"C'mon, Mom. He went to jail for racketeering. What sort of proof do you need?" Tommy "Twinkle Toes" Racatelli also fraternized with many of the big Mafioso guys. "Wait a minute—didn't

Carla Racatelli move to Las Vegas?" I barely knew Carla, but I had attended high school with her grandson, Rocco. Both Carla and Rocco had left town rather suddenly after Tommy's death, without explanation.

Mom nodded and wiped a tear from her eye. "She died a couple of days ago, and we've been summoned."

"Summoned by whom?" Few people held the kind of power to summon the West family. Not even mobsters. The West family was descended from an unbroken lineage of powerful witches. In the supernatural world, we held a certain status. Except for me, of course. While the West name accorded me some respect, my witchy abilities were poor at best. I was a failure in all things involving witchcraft and the supernatural. Special talents brought all sorts of unpredictable things, and I craved a normal life; the kind of carefree existence everyone else seemed to have but me.

Aunt Pearl was another story. Her powers were legendary, and she answered to no one. She was anything but normal, even in the witch world. Few could summon her, and still fewer won her cooperation and respect.

"Carla called for us." Aunt Pearl faced the road ahead so I couldn't read her expression. It was very unlike her to cry, but I thought I heard her sniffle.

"But she's dead now. I don't see how—"

"There's a lot you don't see, Cendrine," Aunt Pearl snapped. "Stop being argumentative."

"But I can't just drop everything and go," I protested.

"You have no choice in the matter. We all must go."

"But if Mrs. Racatelli is already dead, isn't it already too late?" Carla Racatelli had been Aunt Pearl's best friend, right up until her abrupt departure from Westwick Corners. Aunt Pearl hadn't said a word about her since, yet now she was all teary-eyed and hell-bent on attending Carla's funeral. It was strange, to say the least.

"It's never too late to right a wrong. We must wipe out the

Racatelli curse." Mom pulled a tissue from her purse and wiped a tear from her eye. "There are things you don't understand, Cen."

"Try me." I was increasingly frustrated and skeptical that I was getting the truth. I was well aware of the generational gap, but I was twenty-four years old, adult enough to deserve more of an explanation. Curses got way too much credit. That wouldn't go over well in my witch family, but I sincerely believed that there were logical reasons why things went wrong.

Mom shook her head. "Not now, Cen. You'll find out soon enough."

"You're worse than Aunt Pearl. If I'm being kidnapped, I deserve to know why."

"We're going to Carla's funeral and attending to some other business at the same time. That's all I can say right now. We're operating on a need to know basis." Mom glanced at Aunt Pearl in the front passenger seat as she lowered her voice. "I'll tell you more when the time is right. There will be some very interesting people at the funeral."

"If that's supposed to pique my interest, it's not working." I resented Mom's patronizing tone. I also resented her taking Aunt Pearl's side.

"There will be mobsters, Cen. Tough guys who are no match for magic." She smiled.

"Getting mixed up with criminals is a really bad idea, Mom. I'm surprised you're going along with Aunt Pearl." Mom was ultra-cautious and not one to flaunt her powers.

"We're doing a good deed. Somebody needs our help."

"I don't see why I'm needed. You know I couldn't cast a spell if my life depended on it." Aunt Pearl had convinced do-gooder Mom that her supernatural talents were needed, but I couldn't see where I fit in.

I had no urge to save the world, and couldn't even if I tried. I was a witch in name only. I only knew a few spells; nothing of any use against a curse. My only talent was keeping tabs on Aunt Pearl and bailing her out of trouble.

"This will be a good lesson for you. Think of it as fieldwork."

"I'm not ready for that yet. Mixing with mobsters sounds kind of dangerous." I had vowed never to return to Pearl's Charm School to resume my lessons. I just hadn't gotten the nerve to tell my family yet. As far as they knew, I was just taking a semester off from Pearl's Pearls of Wisdom.

Mom gave me a knowing smile but otherwise ignored me.

I sighed. "Aunt Pearl has brainwashed you, can't you see it?" I wasn't getting through to her at all. "Besides, I already have plans tonight."

Aunt Pearl turned around in her seat. "Let's get our priorities straight, missy. We've got to get to Rocco before his enemies do."

"Rocco?" I had almost forgotten about Carla Racatelli's grandson, who at my age was old enough to join the Racatelli family business. It was common knowledge that their import-export business was a front for their shady business activities.

"Yes, Rocco." Mom patted my hand. "He desperately needs our help."

"No." My date with Tyler looked less likely by the minute, and now I'd have to lie to him. I couldn't admit I was a witch on assignment, and I certainly couldn't tell him that I was helping out a mobster. Anger welled up inside of me.

"Now Cen—" Mom started to speak.

"You sure don't need me along."

"Of course I do," Aunt Pearl said. "You're my muscle."

"But I only weigh a few pounds more than you." Aunt Pearl was ninety pounds dripping wet, but I had a few inches on her, so we were pretty much the same build.

Aunt Pearl snorted. "Take a good look at yourself. You're at least twenty pounds heavier than me, maybe more."

"That doesn't make me bodyguard material." I was an occasional gym rat and reasonably fit, but I posed zero threat to mafia wise guys. I swore under my breath. "This is getting more ridiculous by the minute. I demand that you pull over and let me out."

"No can do." Aunt Pearl smirked. "Can't you think about anyone else but yourself for a change?"

"Mom?" Mom could usually talk sense into Aunt Pearl, but she was brainwashed. The funeral had been the trump card.

Mom averted her eyes. Her big sister had either coerced her, put a spell on her, or both. Whatever it was, Mom was fully committed.

I turned to Mom. "You're sure we have no guests arriving?" Business wasn't exactly booming, but we always had at least one or two rooms booked on weekends. We couldn't afford to pass up any income.

"That's the best part, Cen. We'll spend a couple of days in Vegas and be back by Friday in time for our guest arrivals." Mom smiled and leaned back in her swivel chair. "Just kick back and enjoy the ride."

Mom was perpetually over-anxious, but at the moment she seemed so relaxed that I suspected she was on drugs, or worse. I turned to Aunt Pearl. "You put a spell on her. Take it off."

"Relax, Cen. Ruby's overworked and it's high time she had a vacation, and Vegas is the perfect place. What's so bad about helping her relax? Take a chill pill."

"No." I gritted my teeth, determined not to give in.

I was met with silence.

"At least let me use your phone to call *The Shady Creek Tattler* and explain. I can't just blow off a job interview."

"You don't have to. I already called and canceled for you." Aunt Pearl grinned.

"You what?" My face flushed inside the sweltering RV.

"I did you a favor. Face it, Cen. You're not the greatest journalist around."

Aunt Pearl's words stung. She was probably right though. Worst of all, I couldn't use her phone to call Tyler or she'd find out about our secret relationship.

"For the last time, you're coming with us." Aunt Pearl pulled the crumpled ticket from her pocket and waved it in front of me. "My winning ticket is the reason we're able to pay our respects to poor Carla. No magic involved. I won the money fair and square in the state lottery. We'll make a nice vacation out of it."

I rolled my eyes. "Shouldn't you have cashed the ticket first?"

My aunt dismissed me with a wave of her hand. "Plenty of time for that later. I'll redeem it when we get back home."

I met Wilt's gaze in the rear view mirror. Even he looked doubtful.

I turned around in my seat. For the first time I took a good look at the RV interior. It was tastefully decorated and brand new. It had to be worth over a hundred thousand dollars, but I was certain Aunt Pearl's lottery story was a lie. I reached over and tapped her on the shoulder. "What if you made a mistake checking the numbers?"

Silence. Aunt Pearl's selective hearing again.

"Did you kidnap Wilt too? What about his job at the gas station?"

"He works for me now." Aunt Pearl turned around and stared out the window.

"Wilt, pull over and let me out." I hadn't practiced my witchcraft enough to master a teleportation spell, but I could always hitchhike. "I'll catch a ride back to town."

That got Mom's attention, even with Aunt Pearl's spell. "I told you before, you'll do no such thing. Now Pearl, you said Cen had agreed to come."

Aunt Pearl threw her hands in the air, almost knocking Wilt's hand off the steering wheel. "For the last time, we are not pulling over, and you are not hitchhiking. We're all going to Vegas to attend Carla Racatelli's celebration of life." Aunt Pearl paused and hastily added, "Once we pay our respects, I'll consider your request."

The next few minutes were a blur as the RV left the asphalt and rolled onto the gravel shoulder.

CHAPTER 5

The hot asphalt seared my cheek as I regained consciousness. All I saw was gray. My eyes gradually focused on concrete and I realized that I had landed inches away from the cement highway divider.

I had been thrown clear of the RV.

I remained still for a few seconds, stunned. Thankfully nothing was broken, just a lot of painful road rash. I rose to a sitting position, alarmed to find myself in the middle of a four-lane highway. A pickup truck roared by and narrowly missed me as I crawled to the roadside.

"What happened?" The RV lay on its side, partially rolled into a ditch on the opposite side of the highway. It had somehow flipped over the median. The side that faced me was crumpled and dented like it had rolled multiple times.

No one answered.

"Mom? Aunt Pearl?" My heart pounded as I scanned the road for any sign of them or Wilt. I spotted Mom and Aunt Pearl crouched over an unconscious Wilt about fifty yards ahead of the RV. Relief flooded over me as I rose to a standing position. My whole body ached. I took stock of my bruises as I limped over to them.

"This is just one disaster after another," I muttered to myself. Then I caught movement out of the corner of my eye. At first, I thought the RV was moving, but it wasn't. It was slowly turning transparent. Proof positive that the RV was more witchery conjured up by Aunt Pearl.

Her lottery ticket had to be fake too. All I was sure about was Carla Racatelli's funeral. I doubted even Aunt Pearl would lie about her best friend's death. I just hoped we made it to the funeral in one piece.

I was within a few feet, close enough to hear Mom and Aunt Pearl arguing.

"Don't be silly, it's easy to fix," Aunt Pearl said. "I just didn't make the spell long enough."

"You shouldn't be risking our lives like that, Pearl. Don't do it again."

"Stop being such a killjoy and have some fun for a change." Aunt Pearl's eyes locked on mine. "Oh good, I was wondering where you went."

I opened my mouth to answer but Mom shook her head at me. "Help me with Wilt."

Mom shook Wilt's shoulders and his eyes flickered open. "What happened? I don't remember a thing."

"It's all right. We hit a deer."

Wilt rubbed his eyes and rose to a sitting position. "I don't remember that, or rolling the RV."

"You're still groggy. It will come back to you," Mom said.

Wilt slowly stood and scanned the highway. "I don't see the deer."

"He got away." I hated covering for my family, but I felt bad for Wilt. "Let's call someone to tow the RV. Then we can head back home."

Aunt Pearl muttered something in a low voice and the RV gradually solidified. The dents were gone. "Nope. We're road worthy again."

Wilt did a double take. "But I thought—"

"You've had a knock to the head and you're not thinking clearly," Mom said. "Or seeing straight."

"Ruby's right," Aunt Pearl said. "I'll take over the driving for now."

"I am not getting in that thing," I protested. "It's not safe." With Aunt Pearl at the helm, we were headed for trouble and there was no turning back.

"You have to. Everything depends on you, Cen."

"Why me? That makes no sense."

"It makes perfect sense, Cen. You're about to find your calling." Aunt Pearl wrapped her arm around me and gave me a hug.

It was the first hug I remembered from my tough-as-nails aunt in all of my twenty-four years. It should have felt good, but it held a whiff of desperation. Something was up, and I wasn't sure I liked it.

WE ARRIVED at the Hotel Babylon Las Vegas in the early morning, eighteen hours after leaving Westwick Corners. We had driven through the night, stopping only for gas. I was battered, bruised, and broken from the RV crash and Wilt and Aunt Pearl's crazy driving.

And my dress still reeked of gas.

"Cen, just look at this place!" Mom pointed to the expansive marble columns that bordered the lobby and pointed skyward to a multi-story atrium. "This is the Racatelli hotel and casino."

"They own this hotel?" Their reversal of fortune was a far cry from the rented two-bedroom shack and failing scrap metal business they had abandoned in Westwick Corners years earlier.

I had always suspected that the scrap business was a front for Tommy Racatelli's underworld activities. The sudden wealth seemed to prove that the hotel was bought with ill-gotten gains. Unless, like Aunt Pearl, they had gotten an incredibly good stroke of luck.

Whatever the case, Lady Luck had apparently run out. First for Tommy and now Carla. Rocco was probably next. I just hoped he wasn't part of whatever secret mission we were on. He had always taunted me in school, and the more I remembered my annoying classmate, the less I wanted to see him again.

I studied my surroundings while Mom and Aunt Pearl checked us in. The opulent hotel was modeled after a Roman villa, complete with a massive courtyard filled with fountains and hanging gardens. Each floor overlooked the courtyard lobby. Being Vegas, the courtyard wasn't open-air. Thirty-two stories above the courtyard was a glass dome that refracted the sunlight outside. The scenery was meant to keep you inside, not outside.

I shivered in the sterile, air-conditioned lobby as I shuffled past a few bleary-eyed gamblers.

I still had no further details on why we were here. All I was clear on was that I was stuck in Vegas, at least temporarily. I was also hot, hungry and exhausted, and in desperate need of some shut eye. I planned to immediately call Tyler once we had checked in and apologize for standing him up. Then I'd get a few hours' sleep and figure out how to get home, with or without Mom and Aunt Pearl.

CHAPTER 6

I hadn't exactly expected a welcome wagon, but the bullets came as a surprise. They came at us from all directions, the shells ricocheting off the marble columns. I ran towards the exit and collided with two burly men twice my size running in the opposite direction. They wore golf shirts and cargo shorts. They looked like tourists, except for the handguns that they waved in the air. The smaller of the two cursed as he shoved me out of the way.

My shoe caught on the carpet edge and I went down, just as two men in suits came from the opposite direction. They were clearly after the other men and acted like they owned the place.

My heart raced as the men grew closer and the staccato of their footsteps echoed across the marble floor. I froze and debated two equally bad choices: stay still but in plain sight, or dive for cover and tempt a trigger finger.

I crept towards a seating area and crawled under a large mahogany coffee table.

The bullets stopped just as suddenly as they began.

I breathed a sigh of relief until I noticed that both of the casually dressed men were reloading their guns. The suits stopped a few feet from me, their semi-automatics pointed at their adversaries. One of the suits barked a command into a headset and a few seconds later the hotel doors locked.

"Hey! Let me out!" A slight, gray-haired man in jeans and a t-shirt shook the door handle without success. The door didn't budge. He glanced back at the men with a panicked expression. He ducked behind a row of potted palms.

People screamed.

One of the potted palms tipped over and thudded on the marble.

We were trapped in a shootout. I doubted the ceasefire was temporary, but I had no idea what to do next. Panic welled up inside me as I considered my options. I was protected by the coffee table, but my hiding spot was smack dab in the middle of the lobby. I was paralyzed with fear. Any move I made placed me in the line of fire.

The men faced off against each other, just a few feet from my hiding place under the mahogany table. They stood silent for a few seconds, appraising each other. One of the suits whispered something in Italian that I couldn't quite make out.

Someone swore, then all hell broke loose. A lone shot rang out. I couldn't see much from my vantage point, but seconds later, the smaller of the golf shirt guys dropped his gun and went limp. He staggered forward as a crimson stain slowly spread across the waistline of his beige cargo shorts.

His partner grabbed the injured man under one arm and dragged him towards the exit. I froze, unable to move. I was both a witness and an easy target. Mom and Aunt Pearl were nowhere to be seen.

The two suits followed, but kept a ten-foot distance from their casually dressed adversaries. They made no attempt to fire again. If the bullets were a hint to leave, it was a pretty convincing one.

The remotely controlled door swung open and the pursued men disappeared through the open doors.

Once the men had left, the suits reversed course and walked slowly back through the lobby. They spoke in low voices, but the cavernous lobby magnified their conversation. They chatted about last night's heavyweight fight, as if the shootout that had just happened was the most ordinary thing in the world.

I flashed back to Carla Racatelli as I peered out from my vantage point under the heavy table. Given the family's underworld ties, I wondered if the shootout was somehow related to Carla's death. That seemed much more likely than the curse Mom and Aunt Pearl spoke of.

Vegas or not, I had no intention of pressing my luck by attending the funeral. The hotel itself was unsafe, and I was certain the funeral would be even more so. I had to do everything in my power to stop Mom and Aunt Pearl from whatever their quest was. Sometimes it was best not to tempt fate.

I had to get us back to Westwick Corners, and there was no time to waste.

CHAPTER 7

I saw no one else other than the gunmen in the lobby. Mom, Aunt Pearl, Wilt and the others were nowhere to be seen. If other people hid behind the heavy furniture and marble columns, I couldn't see them. They had either hidden just as the shooting started, or they had escaped via the stairs or elevators.

I held my breath as footsteps sounded on the marble floor. An unarmed man strode towards the suits. He came from the direction of the elevators, though I hadn't noticed him before. He acted as if a hotel lobby shootout was an everyday occurrence. I watched him walk by from my vantage point under the table. He wore black jeans, an expensive-looking white linen shirt that clung to his muscled torso, and a self-assured smirk that said he was the boss.

He was the type of arrogant guy I despised, but I found it hard to take my eyes off him. He was tall, dark, and oddly familiar. He abruptly stopped and turned his head in my direction. My heart thumped as his steel blue eyes locked on mine.

Caught.

I retreated further under the table and sucked in my breath. My life was about to be over before it even began. This turf war was almost certainly his, and he wouldn't want to leave any witnesses.

After what seemed like an eternity, he broke his gaze and resumed walking in the same direction as the suits. He kicked the dropped revolver with a calfskin boot, sending it clattering across the marble floor towards me. It landed inches from my hiding spot.

The barrel pointed towards me and I thanked my lucky stars that the gun hadn't fired from the impact. I held my breath, scared that one of the men would retrieve the gun and discover me under the table.

The man joined the suits by the front door. The two men were clearly under his command. The boss man paused and turned. His eyes scanned the lobby once more before turning back to me.

The man had somehow noticed me, despite my hiding place. I felt exposed and vulnerable, as if the table wasn't there to cover me. On the other hand, he had made no effort to expose me, so I let down my guard a little.

I also felt a surge of adrenaline, and something else I couldn't quite describe. My strange attraction to him was almost enough to draw me out of hiding. As I angled my body under the table to keep him in my line of sight, I hit my head on the underside of the table.

"Damn!" The table sent shockwaves through my head as my voice carried through the silent lobby.

The boss man frowned. Seconds later he turned without a word and whisked the suits through the heavy glass doors, which were now unlocked. One of the men went ahead, followed by the hunky boss man.

The last man remaining tracked his gun around the lobby in a semi-circle to prevent anyone from following. After what seemed like an eternity, he left the building. Seconds later car doors slammed and tires screeched into the distance.

A split second of silence soon erupted into panicked screams and shouts. I wasn't alone in the lobby after all. People scrambled from their hiding places and raced around the lobby looking for loved ones.

I stayed under the table, in shock from both the shooting and my attraction to the handsome stranger. I opened my mouth but no sound came out. I was a mess.

"Ouch!" Someone kicked my ankle and I rolled over to face Aunt Pearl. I was positive she hadn't been under the table seconds earlier.

"Let me go home, Aunt Pearl. This is like a bad movie, only it's real. What the hell just happened?" I couldn't fathom any other reason for gunfire at our five-star hotel.

Aunt Pearl frowned as she crawled out from underneath the table.

Panic rose in my gut as I searched for Mom and Wilt. They had stood beside me seconds before the shooting broke out, but were now nowhere in sight. I broke into a sweat as police sirens wailed outside. I inched towards the table edge and peered out from my hiding spot as the sirens grew louder.

People were everywhere, some crying, others huddled together in shock. A dozen or so people pushed and shoved towards the exit, oblivious to the fact they were following in the footsteps of the recently departed gunmen.

I slowly slid out from under the table and rose to a sitting position. I was reluctant to stray far from my refuge just yet. A woman beside me shouted frantically into her cell phone while others crammed into elevators, anxious to escape to the safety of their rooms upstairs.

I spotted Mom as she rose from behind a large overstuffed couch. Wilt stood beside her. Relieved, I glanced back at Aunt Pearl. She sat upright and cross-legged on the thick throw rug a few feet from the table. Her hands rested on her thighs in a Zen-like yoga pose, as if deep in meditation amidst the chaos.

But I knew better. She was casting a spell of some sort. I held out my hand, which she promptly brushed away.

"Darn it, we missed him."

"Missed who?" I asked. "What the heck is going on that you're not telling me?" The lobby swarmed with at least a dozen police by now. They directed people towards a line by the reception desk, where they interviewed witnesses one by one. There were officers stationed at the exits and elevators, so no one else could leave the lobby. It was just a matter of time before they questioned us.

"Did you see that handsome fella?" Aunt Pearl's eyes widened in mock innocence.

I shrugged, afraid to say anything that might reveal my attraction.

"It's obvious you did, judging from your reaction. That was Carla's grandson Rocco." Aunt Pearl smirked. "How could you not recognize our Rocco after all these years? You two used to play together all the time when you were kids. Remember?" Aunt Pearl gazed wistfully into space.

"The guy was most definitely not Rocco." I hadn't seen Rocco since high school, but my former schoolmate bore no resemblance to the mysterious, attractive man who had powered by us. I knew, because I had gotten a *very* good look at him. The mystery man was unforgettable.

I stood and walked over to the sofa behind me and surveyed the lobby. Aside from the gaggle of stunned tourists, there was little evidence of the shooting. Just a few bullet holes in the lobby walls, which the police were busy attending to.

It was nothing short of amazing that no one had been hit in the crossfire. "We need to talk to the police. We're witnesses."

"Don't be silly, Cen. We can't draw attention to ourselves. Rocco does enough of that already. Such a flair for the dramatic." Aunt Pearl tittered as her hand flew to her mouth. "I do wish he would tone it down a bit though. Manny's not going to like it."

I doubted that the police would let us leave without interviewing us, but things were still pretty chaotic in the lobby.

"What's so funny? We just got shot at. We need to get out of here." I wanted to ask who Manny was, but Aunt Pearl was clearly baiting me, and I had no intention of giving her the satisfaction of asking.

Aunt Pearl shook her head. "You're right. Let's dump our luggage upstairs and then go to the casino. You need to unwind. Maybe we'll even see Rocco."

"He's the last person I want to see right now." That was true and not so true. I could stare at that man forever. But I wasn't about to be a pawn in one of Aunt Pearl's escapades. I also didn't want to reconnect with a boy from my past that I had never even liked very much. No matter how good he looked.

"Stop being so negative." Aunt Pearl rolled her eyes. "You complained about the gas and your stupid job interview all the way here."

"Why wouldn't I? You tricked me into coming here."

Aunt Pearl waved her hand in dismissal. "Poor Rocco just lost his Grandma and all you think about is you. I never should have brought you along."

"That's right. You shouldn't have. I want nothing to do with Rocco and whatever weird scheme you've concocted." My mood lightened a little as Mom and Wilt walked over and joined us in the seating area.

Aunt Pearl grinned an evil grin. "Rocco's not just a nice boy, Cen. He's ambitious and smart. You two would make quite a pair."

"I don't see what that has to do with anything." The idea of Aunt Pearl fixing me up with Rocco while he was still mourning his grandmother was extremely tacky, even for her. I just hoped she wouldn't do anything to embarrass me.

"Oh, but you will, Cen." A smile played across my aunt's lips as she placed an arm around me and squeezed my shoulder. "You will."

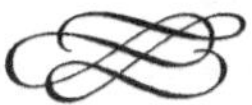

 e checked in once the Las Vegas police had taken our eyewitness accounts and personal details. I was completely exhausted, though it was barely after breakfast.

I was furious with Aunt Pearl for the way she danced around the truth. "Why didn't you tell the police that you knew Rocco?"

"They never asked, so why mention it? It makes no difference either way."

I shook my head. "It makes a huge difference. He was with two of the shooters."

"Whatever." Aunt Pearl dismissed me with a wave. "We've got a life or death job to do, so we need to stay under the radar."

"What job?"

Aunt Pearl made a zipping motion across her lips and turned away. She completely ignored me as we followed the bellhop and our luggage across the lobby to the elevators, zigzagging around groups of bewildered guests.

The only saving grace from the chaotic lobby scene was that Wilt soon disappeared. He had decided to stay in the RV instead of the one suite we were apparently all supposed to share. I was relieved, since even reluctant witches like me had to let their hair down and be their witchy selves once in a while.

That would have been impossible with Wilt in the suite, and my temper was already frayed from our exhausting road trip. One of us was bound to slip up sooner or later. Hiding witchy talents 24/7 was almost harder than being a witch in the first place.

The bellhop motioned us towards a private elevator at the end of the elevator bank. The doors opened and we stepped inside the elevator like VIPs, attracting glares from the dozens of people lined up at the regular elevators. Our special treatment almost certainly came with strings attached.

The bellhop followed us inside the elevator, pulling his brass and velvet-lined luggage cart behind him. He scanned his key card and pressed one of several buttons that were marked with letters instead of floor numbers. He pressed a button engraved with an "R" written in fancy script.

I was surprised to see my suitcase atop the luggage heap. I hadn't packed anything for my unexpected trip. Either Aunt Pearl had brought my luggage because she had planned to kidnap me all along, or she had used magic.

I barely had time to wonder before the elevator door opened into a spacious marble foyer with impossibly high ceilings. It was in the same Italian theme as the lobby but on a smaller scale. The walls were lined with large impressionist paintings above a marble fountain with colored water that burbled.

Mom exited the elevator and gawked at her surroundings. "You sure this is the right room? It looks more like a villa."

The décor was a cross between a French provincial apartment and a mid-century Italian villa that was undergoing some weird nineteen seventies' renovation. There were a lot of other decorating themes mixed in, but those were the main ones. Like the lobby, it was a blend of several different eras.

The ornate European architecture contrasted with gold-colored shag carpeting. Smack dab in the middle of the open floor plan was a sunken living room seating area, straight out of an old 1970s Mary Tyler Moore sitcom. A wrought-iron spiral staircase led to a second floor, where I assumed the bedrooms were.

The over-the-top interior decorating made me momentarily forget that we were in a brand new Las Vegas high-rise and not a retro, hippie Versailles. I stood in the foyer, awestruck.

"C'mon, we haven't got all day." Aunt Pearl grabbed my arm and pulled me into the suite. "We've got stuff to take care of."

I wrested my arm from hers and paused at one of the large oil paintings. Judging from the brushstrokes and expensive-looking frame, the painting was both authentic and really old.

The portrait looked to be from the 1930s. A small man in a pinstriped suit stood behind a seated woman. Her sequined dress was accentuated by a long string of pearls. She had the same piercing blue eyes as the man in the lobby.

I traced my hand across the bottom of the frame. It slid slightly out of place so I righted it. It was the first suite I had stayed in where the pictures weren't bolted to the wall. But there was something else. In place of one of the man's eyes was a bullet hole.

I gasped and turned to Mom and Aunt Pearl, but they had already left the foyer. I followed them into the suite and watched the bellhop take our bags up the spiral staircase.

"Welcome!" a deep male voice boomed behind me.

I jumped and turned to see a fit-looking blond man in his early thirties, formally dressed in a dark suit. My first thought was that he was dressed for the funeral.

He smiled and extended his hand. "I'm Christophe, your butler."

I frowned as I shook his hand. I scanned the suite. It had to be over two thousand square feet just on the main floor, plus the additional space on the upper floor. "I think there's been a mistake. This isn't our room."

Christophe smiled politely but didn't respond.

"We can't afford to stay in a place like this." Mom turned to Pearl. "It must cost a small fortune. Exactly how much did you win in the lottery?"

Aunt Pearl waved her hand in dismissal. "Don't worry about it. I'll tell you later."

"Can I offer you ladies some cocktails?" Christophe asked.

"It's barely 9 a.m.," I said. "Don't you think it's a bit early?" Butler-prepared drinks had to be several magnitudes more expensive than mini-bar drinks. Even if Aunt Pearl's lottery win was real, I doubted we could afford it.

"There's no time like the present." Mom giggled. "Live a little, Cen."

I grabbed Aunt Pearl's boney arm and pulled her aside. "What did you give to Mom? I've never seen her like this."

"Relax. She's finally enjoying herself for a change, instead of working herself to exhaustion at that stupid inn."

"You want our bed and breakfast to fail. That's the real reason you brought both of us here." It was no secret that my aunt resented our bed and breakfast business venture back in Westwick Corners. I glanced back at Mom, who stood at the bar where Christophe placed the finishing touches on three fruity-looking drinks.

Aunt Pearl took one and headed towards French doors that led to the patio.

Mom grabbed one and downed half of it in one gulp. "This man is a genius. I wish we could hire you to work at our inn."

Christophe smiled. "Maybe you can. I'll be out of a job soon, and I'm tired of Vegas. Tell me about your inn."

"Oh, it's nothing as grand as the Hotel Babylon. The Westwick Corners Inn only has twelve rooms. And it's located in an almost-ghost town." Mom giggled as she finished the rest of her drink. "Too dull for a young man like you. I feel silly even mentioning it."

Christophe took her glass and headed to the bar for a refill.

Mom followed close behind.

I headed out onto the patio and joined Aunt Pearl. The large wraparound penthouse patio was almost as large as the suite itself. It had its own lap pool, a hot tub, and seating arranged to maximize the city view, which probably looked magnificent by night. At this early hour everything was still quiet, like half the city was still asleep.

I turned to my aunt. "Mom's right. There's no way we can afford this place, even at a deep discount."

"Relax," said Aunt Pearl. "This might be the high roller suite, but it doesn't cost us a penny."

I turned to face my aunt. "We're not high rollers, and we can't stay here for nothing. What's the catch?"

"No catch." Aunt Pearl winked.

Mom emerged from the suite, as if on cue. She walked unsteadily past me, spilling her refilled glass on the concrete deck. "Nothing is free, because the hotel expects us to spend thousands of dollars gambling. Even your lottery winnings might not be enough. In fact, it could be a disaster."

Mom was alluding to Aunt Pearl's gambling problem. The lottery winnings were a double-edged sword. I doubted my aunt would steer clear of the slots and tables for long.

"I didn't spend a dime on the suite, or anything else. Rocco comped the room for us because he considers us family. Not that I can't afford this. Besides, I can gamble if I want to. I'm a millionaire and I've got money to burn."

I flashed back to the wise guy and the lobby gunfight. I didn't like owing favors to a guy who needed bodyguards. Aunt Pearl had probably misinterpreted his invitation, if there even was one in the first place. I made a mental note to check in at the front desk later on to confirm our room rate.

Mom pointed an index finger at Pearl. "I still think we should've stayed in the RV. You're on the hook for the bill if anything goes wrong." She headed towards the deck chairs without waiting for a response.

Aunt Pearl turned to me and rolled her eyes. "You both need to stop worrying and enjoy yourselves."

"How can we? You tricked both of us into coming on your magical mystery tour, and you're pretty vague about how and when exactly you won the lottery. I'm not relaxing until you tell me what's really going on." I almost felt like joining Wilt in the RV. Almost, but not quite.

"Okay, fine. I'll tell you, but you can't tell Ruby." Aunt Pearl massaged her temples. "It's kind of complicated. I don't even know where to start."

"How about explaining the lobby shootout for starters?"

Aunt Pearl's hand flew to her mouth. "Wasn't that terrible? I have no idea how that happen—"

I held up my hand in protest. "I think you know exactly what's going on, and if you don't tell me, I'm leaving. I'll find my own way home." It seemed that she had planned everything all along, as a lead-in to the overly dramatic confession she was about to give. "I'll rent a car or something."

"How? You forgot your purse and you've got no money."

"I'll figure something out."

"If you practiced your witchcraft you could conjure one up. Such a waste of talent." Aunt Pearl shook her head slowly.

"Quit changing the subject, Aunt Pearl."

"Okay, fine." She sighed. "What do you want to know?"

"Everything. Starting with the guys downstairs. You know something you're not telling." Either she was somehow involved or knew more than she let on.

Aunt Pearl dabbed an imaginary tear from her eye. "I wasn't going to tell anyone, but to be honest, it will be a relief to have a confidante. Someone on my side."

"I never said anything about being on your side. I just want to know what you've gotten us mixed up in."

"They've already taken Carla, and Tommy before her." Aunt Pearl sucked in her breath. "They'll get Rocco too, unless we can stop them. I have a plan."

I covered my ears. "*We* are not stopping anybody. Does Mom know any of this?"

"There's some things she's better off not knowing."

"Like?"

"Family secrets," Aunt Pearl said. "This one will break Ruby's heart."

CHAPTER 9

$\mathcal{I}$ gulped my fruity drink. Aunt Pearl's claim defied belief. I couldn't recall Mom ever even dating, let alone having a serious relationship. And she had no reason to have kept it a secret from me.

Dad had disappeared without a trace when I was in grade school. Since then, Mom had immersed herself in cooking, baking, and gardening. She even made wine from our estate vineyard and had turned our ancestral home into a boutique bed and breakfast. She kept herself busy, never mentioning Dad. She never mentioned any dates or a steady boyfriend either.

Yet Aunt Pearl claimed otherwise. "Ruby was jilted by her lover. He dumped Ruby for Carla Racatelli."

"What lover? You're making all this up." Mom hadn't left Westwick Corners since I could remember, and she'd had no suitors that I was aware of. She was too much of a homebody to lead a double life. But my aunt seemed serious. I didn't think she was lying this time.

Aunt Pearl slowly shook her head. "I wish I was making it up. If only I could undo everything that's happened. But I can't. Let's go back inside where we can talk without Ruby overhearing."

I followed reluctantly, stunned at the possibility of Mom in a secret relationship. I was also a little hurt that she had to keep secrets from me. "Why didn't Mom tell me about this guy? When did she ever see him?"

"She's a witch, Cen. A competent witch has many methods at her disposal to be in more than one place at the same time. If you practiced your spells more often, you would know that." Aunt Pearl frowned. "Ruby knew you wouldn't approve of her affair, so she never told you. You're so straight-laced and moral."

"Since when is that a bad thing?" I sat down in an oversized armchair, kitty corner to Aunt Pearl, who perched on the edge of an impossibly long, white leather sofa.

"I never said it was. But Ruby knew you'd get all judge-y on her."

"I am *not* judge-y." The thought of Mom having a love life had never even occurred to me. I guess I should have expected her to date eventually, and it had been decades since Dad left. She just never seemed interested in a relationship, and she wasn't one for secrets. There had to be more to the story. And, apparently, there was.

"Ruby should be glad to be rid of that bum." Aunt Pearl leaned back against the arm of the sofa, her skinny legs stretched out in front of her. "Who knows, it could have been her instead."

I gulped. "You think he killed Carla? Who is this guy?"

"Bones Battilana. One of the most powerful mob bosses in America. He wanted to move in on Las Vegas, but all of Nevada is controlled by the Racatellis. Rumor has it that Bones knocked off Tommy a few years back to wrest control from the Racatelli family. He never expected Carla to take over the reins. She turned out to be better at business than Tommy ever was. So his plan to consolidate power backfired."

"Then he romanced Carla instead?" Realization slowly dawned

on me. "You're saying that Mom dated a mobster, and then he dumped her to move in on Carla? That's crazy."

"It kind of looks that way. I just don't know what to do." Aunt Pearl threw her hands up in the air, spilling her fruity cocktail all over the sofa. "Now you see why I need your help. I don't want her to freak out at the funeral when she sees Bones."

"I guess you'd better break the news to her soon." My fruity drink packed a powerful punch. I felt drunk, and I had taken barely more than a few sips. In fact, they seemed to be affecting all of us to the extreme. It seemed a little paranoid, but I was beginning to wonder if they contained something more than alcohol.

Christophe appeared seconds later with a cloth and a bottle of Club Soda. Within a minute he had expertly blotted away the spilled drink. He beamed proudly, reminding me of a masculine Martha Stewart, just waiting for a chance to show off his many tricks.

Christophe made a slight bow and turned in the direction of the kitchen. We sat in silence until he was out of earshot.

"You know, Cen…you have a very good way of dealing with crises." Aunt Pearl scratched her chin as if considering my talents— or lack thereof—for the very first time. "This is a very delicate matter, and you're so much better at these things than I am."

"No. How am I supposed to tell Mom something I'm not even supposed to know in the first place?"

"You'll figure it out." She scanned the suite to ensure no one was listening. Her voice dropped to a whisper. "Bones Battilana is a pretty big deal around here. We have to keep this on the down-low."

"I think you're just making all this up. Mom would never in a million years date a mobster, let alone some guy named 'Bones.'" Mom dating a guy named after body parts gave me the creeps.

"Ruby might be your mom, but she's no different than any other woman. She's been involved with him for almost a decade. We all have needs, Cen. Even I do."

This was getting weirder by the minute. It was hard enough

imagining Mom with a man, but the idea of grumpy Aunt Pearl having "needs" just seemed at odds with both her personality and lifestyle. She had never married and seemed always to have a hate-on for anyone with a Y chromosome.

"This guy must have a real name."

"Danny. Everything seemed just fine until about three weeks ago. That's when Bones—I mean Danny—told Ruby he had to go on a month-long business trip to Asia. She hasn't seen him since. She thinks everything between them is just fine. In reality, he just dumped her for Carla, but didn't have the guts to tell her to her face."

"And now Carla's dead. Talk about bad timing."

"Or maybe good timing. I'm almost positive Bones killed Carla," Aunt Pearl said. "That's why I've assigned you to *Project Vegas Vendetta*. We need to investigate Carla's murder and avenge her death. Oh...and your first task is to tell Ruby what her no-good boyfriend's been up to."

At least Mom's ex-boyfriend was an "ex", but the thought that he might be Carla's suspected killer made my hair stand up. I knew next to nothing about Carla's death, but there just had to be another explanation. I jumped as the French doors swung open and Mom returned inside. "We're doing no such thing!"

"Huh?" Mom grinned at us from the doorway. She swayed on her feet as she raised her empty glass and toasted us. She rarely drank, and I had never even seen her drunk before. Today seemed to be a first for a lot of things, none of them good.

"It'll be so much better coming from you than me. You know I'll screw things up." Aunt Pearl shifted on the sofa and brought her knees up to her chest. She fake-smiled at me. "Please?"

Aunt Pearl never took no for an answer, and there would be definite consequences for me unless I agreed to her plan. I felt like I was backed into a corner. "You never said Carla was murdered. Does Mom know that part?"

Mom twirled her cocktail glass and walked unsteadily past us towards the kitchen in search of Christophe and his magical elixir.

Aunt Pearl waited until she had left the room. "Yes."

"You should have told me all this a long time ago."

"What can I say? Ruby's relationship was her secret, and she swore me to secrecy." Aunt Pearl raised her hands, palms outward. Her bottom lip trembled. "I know, Cen. Bad decision on my part. But it's a little late to fix that now. You know how bad I am at this stuff. I'll botch it and make Ruby even more upset. She has no clue about his affair. She'll be heartbroken. She thought Bones was about to propose to her."

"Danny."

Aunt Pearl rolled her eyes. "Okay. Danny."

Another bombshell. "The shootout in the lobby…was that part of Battilana's business trip?"

Aunt Pearl nodded. "Rocco's men were defending him against another Bones Battilana hit. We've got to get to them before they get to Rocco. That's why you have to tell Ruby about his illicit affair with Carla. We can't risk her going near him while he's so dangerous and unpredictable."

"The police haven't arrested him yet?"

Aunt Pearl shook her head. "He's playing the grieving husband, and the police are going along with it. The husband's always the number one suspect, though. In the meantime, he carries on as usual, trying to gain control of Carla's holdings. That's why he married her in the first place. He couldn't wrest control of Las Vegas from the Racatellis, so he joined them instead. Now he's in on the action."

"Whoa—Bones is married to Carla now?" My head spun from everything Aunt Pearl had just said. "How much do I tell Mom?"

"All of it. With Carla gone, Ruby might try to reconcile with him. That would be a grave mistake. While you're doing that, I'll get us some more stiff drinks." Aunt Pearl sprung off the couch and went in search of our butler. "Christophe? Yoo-hoo!"

I jumped up after her. "Wait—you need to fill the police in on what you know before they come asking. Maybe they can protect Mom." My head spun with my aunt's claims. My missed interview seemed inconsequential now.

"No can do, Cen. We trust no one. Not even the police."

CHAPTER 10

$\mathcal{I}$ stepped out of the elevator, still dazed from Aunt Pearl's confession. I also felt the effects of Christophe's powerful cocktails. I had lost count of how many I had, though I hadn't intended to drink a single one. As for Aunt Pearl, I was unsure whether to be scared or angry. I felt a little of both.

I headed across the lobby towards the casino. It wasn't exactly hard to find with all the flashing lights, bells, and hordes of overweight, middle-aged tourists. Most wore Las Vegas t-shirts and shorts. The contrast between the casual dress and opulent decor jarred my senses.

Of course, casinos turned away no one. Especially not people with money in their pockets, no matter how poorly dressed. And from what I could see, business was booming.

I refocused on my mission: finding a phone to call Tyler to apologize for our missed date. I considered a flight home, but without money and credit cards, that was impossible. At any rate, Aunt Pearl would thwart my efforts. She wanted me at the funeral at any cost and wouldn't take no for an answer.

I couldn't locate a lobby phone, and the only hotel equipment with a ring tone were the slot machines. The whole atmosphere jarred my already confused senses. There were no windows or clocks. Without a watch, it was impossible to tell the time of day. Anything that distracted gamblers was considered a no-no.

I headed through the lobby and exited the revolving glass doors onto the street. The sky was slightly overcast, but it had no impact on the heat that already assaulted my air-conditioned skin. I guessed that it was probably still late morning, though I had lost all sense of time.

I stood a few feet to the side of the entrance and took a few moments to get my bearings. I headed towards what looked like a shopping district, hoping to find a mall or a store where I could buy a cheap throwaway cell phone.

Tyler must be wondering why I hadn't called him after missing our date last night. I had probably blown any chance I ever had with him.

First I would call Tyler, and then I would find a way to get back home. The easiest and fastest mode of travel involved magical intervention, but my magic skills weren't good enough to muster anything close to teleportation. I seriously doubted that either Mom or Aunt Pearl would help me. At the very least, they would point out my lapsed magic lessons and claim that it served me right.

I debated how much to tell Tyler. I wanted him to understand that I hadn't just casually canceled our date. Except my kidnapping story sounded simply unbelievable. Telling the truth would only worsen his already bad impression of Aunt Pearl.

Two blocks later I saw no sign of retail stores or anywhere else to buy a cell phone. The only businesses on the strip seemed to be other casinos. My lack of familiarity with Las Vegas meant it could take me a long time to find a phone.

I stood on the corner, uncertain and frustrated on what to do next. Then it dawned on me that I had other options. While my witchcraft talents weren't adequate to transport myself back to

Westwick Corners, I knew basic spellcasting and had conjured up inanimate objects before. Never a cell phone, but it was probably within my abilities. I wished I had at least practiced, so my skills wouldn't be so rusty.

Instead, I had squandered the very advantage that could have gotten me out of my current situation. While I could blame Aunt Pearl for kidnapping me, the mess I was in was really my fault in the end.

I had only recently decided that my natural talents weren't cheating at all. In fact, they weren't talents, since every spell took hours to learn, and a significant amount of practice to keep up my knowledge. I got out of it what I put in. Nothing more, and nothing less.

This epiphany came to me when I made a bet with Aunt Pearl— and lost. Losing the bet had committed me to all seventy-two lessons in her Pearls of Wisdom course at Pearl's Charm School. The curriculum encompassed everything one needed to become a successful witch. Unfortunately, I had only progressed to lesson three. That meant I was pretty good at getting rid of things, but less successful at conjuring things up.

But I had conjured up a few small things. My results often had unintended consequences, but at least they amounted to something. It was worth a shot.

I massaged my temples as I tried to recall the exact words of the Small Objects spell I had learned in lesson two. Fragments of the spell slowly came back to me as I pictured the words in my mind.

I changed direction and headed back to the hotel. I could practice in my bedroom in the suite without Mom or Aunt Pearl's knowledge. At least they would be nearby if I ran into trouble.

One, two, three,
Cell phone come to me...

. . .

No, that didn't seem right. My pace slowed to a crawl.

One, two, three,
  Cell phone make it be...

A ONE-WORD MIX-UP could have disastrous results, so trial and error wasn't really an option. If only I had an example to refer to.

I entered the lobby and headed for the elevator. I was so lost in thought that I ran smack into a man's chest.

A muscular, hard chest.

And stared straight into the intense blue eyes of a man I hadn't seen in a very long time.

CHAPTER 11

I pulled back and started to apologize, suddenly embarrassed.

"Cendrine West! I'd know you anywhere." Rocco Racatelli stared at my chest before slowly raising his gaze to my face.

"Fancy meeting you here." I resented the ogling, until I realized that I had done the exact same thing. I studied his expression, unsure if he was joking or serious. According to Aunt Pearl, Rocco not only knew we were here but had arranged our fancy high-roller suite. The last person I wanted to owe favors to was Rocco Racatelli.

"You're surprised to see me?" I flashed back to the lobby shootout. He had definitely noticed me this morning, though in the hours since then, I was slightly more disheveled and noticeably tipsy.

Based on Aunt Pearl's claims, our meetup could hardly be considered a coincidence if he was expecting us. But Aunt Pearl told a lot of white lies, so it was impossible to know for sure. I kept my mouth shut, just in case.

"Of course." His blue eyes twinkled. "How long has it been? Ten years?"

I met his gaze and nodded, speechless at this handsome stranger who looked nothing like the Rocco I remembered. Gone was the chubby pimple-faced teenager I had known in Westwick Corners. A decade and time at the gym had dramatically transformed Rocco's appearance. He had changed into casual attire since the lobby shoot-out, but still looked sharp. Muscles rippled under a tight white t-shirt that was almost as bright as his brilliant smile. He wore faded blue jeans and cowboy boots. His tanned face already sported a touch of five o'clock shadow.

And those piercing blue eyes. I couldn't quite meet his gaze, but I couldn't turn away either. I felt completely under his spell.

I opened my mouth to answer, but nothing came out. It wasn't just his handsome appearance that had me speechless. He seemed to have an aura that attracted me like a magnet. My heart fluttered in my chest and I flushed all over.

I fought the strange urge to pull him closer and burrow my face into his well-defined chest. My common sense held me back, but just barely. This was definitely not the same Rocco I grew up with in Westwick Corners.

Wow.

What the hell was going on? It was like I was under a spell or something.

Or under the influence of Aunt Pearl's witchery.

If Rocco noticed my awkward silence, he didn't let on.

"Let's grab a drink and catch up." Rocco's eyes darted back and forth as he checked out the crowded street.

"Uh, I can't right now, Rocco. I was just on my way out to buy a cell phone." My heart pounded in my chest as a thin sheen of sweat broke out on my forehead. "Know where I can get one?"

"You need to call someone? Here, use mine." He unlocked the screen and passed it to me.

I almost handed his phone back before I thought better of it. It could take me hours to either buy or conjure up a phone. Using his phone immediately solved my problem. The sooner I called Tyler, the better. "Sure, thanks. I'll just be a minute."

I walked a few feet away to a garden seating area and punched in Tyler's number. Rocco walked back towards the hotel entrance and motioned for me to follow. I trailed behind him as he headed towards a bar just off the lobby. I pretty much had to follow him, now that I had his phone.

Tyler answered on the first ring. "I figured something must have happened. Where are you?"

It felt so good just to hear his voice, and he didn't seem angry at all. Instead, he sounded concerned. Very sweet considering I had stood him up.

"Uh, Las Vegas." I glanced at Rocco, who was a few feet away and out of earshot. He was in the bar, flagging down a server. "I guess Aunt Pearl wasn't kidding about the trip." I omitted my missed job interview and Aunt Pearl's winning lottery ticket. All that was far too hard to explain, and I didn't have much time to talk since I was on Rocco's phone. "I'm really sorry about our date. I don't blame you if you're mad at me."

Tyler chuckled softly. "Things happen. Especially with that aunt of yours. We'll just reschedule. When will you be back in town?"

"Uh...I'm not sure yet. We're here for a funeral, only Aunt Pearl won't tell me how long we're here for." I omitted all mention of Aunt Pearl's *Project Vegas Vendetta* and the lobby shootout. The former was unexplainable, and the latter was bound to freak him out.

"Oh? Who died?"

"Carla Racatelli, an old friend of Aunt Pearl's. Her death was rather sudden." It sounded better than saying she was murdered.

Tyler sucked in his breath, and then the line went silent.

Doubt crept into my thoughts. Maybe Tyler was mad after all. What if he didn't want another date? "Are you still there?"

Tyler cleared his throat. "Racatelli? As in Tommy and Carla Racatelli?"

"Uh-huh. You know them?"

"No, but I know of them. You must know them well, to travel all the way to Vegas for the funeral."

"They lived in Westwick Corners about ten years ago. I went to school with their grandson, Rocco. He was raised by Carla and Tommy after his parents died in a car accident when he was a toddler." Of course, Tyler wouldn't know that, since he had only moved to Westwick Corners a few months ago when he accepted the sheriff's job.

Only he did know. He knew more about them than I did, and spent the next ten minutes telling me.

"Rocco's parents didn't die in a car accident, Cen. They were shot in their car. They were murdered, execution-style."

My pulse quickened. "You're sure about that?"

"Of course I'm sure. It was a mob hit. I'm surprised you didn't know already. Westwick Corners is so small. I wouldn't have thought it would stay secret for long."

"I guess it did." Small towns were notoriously bad for keeping secrets, except for the few that could tear people apart. Those tended to stay hidden forever. Mob business apparently fit into that category. I wondered what else my family hadn't told me.

My face flushed as I glanced over at Rocco, oblivious to my conversation about his family. Luckily, he didn't meet my gaze, or I wouldn't have been able to think straight. The strange hold he had over me seemed to weaken with a little distance. Another sign that it was witchcraft at work.

"Cen?"

"Huh?"

"Please be careful. You know about their family business, right?"

I nodded, which was silly because Tyler was miles away and couldn't see me. "The Racatellis had a bootlegging business during

Prohibition, and Tommy was involved in some political scandal and kickbacks and stuff. All that ended with his accidental death ten years ago."

"There's a lot more to it than that, Cen. You remember how Tommy Racatelli died?"

"Car accident. He missed a hairpin turn and went over a cliff." I frowned. "Either the Racatellis are really bad drivers or they have the worst luck with cars."

"Tommy's accident was a hit ordered by a rival crime boss. Twinkletoes Racatelli was a powerful man."

"Twinkletoes? Never heard that nickname before." I vaguely remembered the single car accident that took Rocco's grandfather. It had seemed strange at the time since Mr. Racatelli had cataracts and never drove after dark.

"Racatelli kept his business and personal life very separate. That's why he lived in a sleepy town like Westwick Corners. These wise guys are dangerous, Cen."

"Not anymore, since he's dead."

"No, but his associates are alive and kicking. You know Carla was part of the family business too, right? Her grandson Rocco almost certainly is too."

"Rocco?" It felt weird to be talking about him while using his phone. "I doubt it."

"Just be very careful if you're around him. Better yet, stay away. If someone takes him out, you could be collateral damage."

I flashed back to the lobby shootout. Tyler had a point. With Carla gone, Rocco was the sole surviving Racatelli. I didn't know for certain Rocco was a criminal, but it begged a little fact-checking. "I'll be careful, but there's really nothing to worry about." I was secretly pleased by Tyler's concern.

"They're mobsters, Cen. Carla ran a pretty big organization. If she's gone, you can bet there's a power struggle already underway to gain control of the business."

"How do you know so much about them?"

"I'm a cop, remember? I also worked undercover. The Racatellis were—and are—a pretty big deal. Keep away if you can."

Despite Tyler's warnings, I didn't have much choice in the matter. I omitted any mention of Rocco and the lobby shootout as I debated the logic of borrowing Rocco's phone. "I'll be fine. Our families aren't all that close. Aunt Pearl was friends with Carla, so she just wants to pay her respects."

"Just be careful. Call me if you have any worries at all."

"Okay." I promised to call Tyler after the funeral. Aunt Pearl's commitments would be wrapped up and we could head back home.

Suddenly everything made sense. A small town like Westwick Corners was the perfect place to operate a criminal enterprise. Nobody could come and go without the whole town knowing. It was like an early warning system, though in the end it had failed the Racatellis. Even the sheriff could be bought, or if not, scared off.

Another shattered illusion from childhood.

How much did Mom and Aunt Pearl know that they weren't letting on? If Aunt Pearl knew any of Carla's business secrets, she could be a target too. Knowledge could be a very dangerous thing.

CHAPTER 12

I said goodbye to Tyler just as Rocco waved me over to his corner table. He sat with his back to the wall, giving him a clear view of anyone entering or exiting the bar. He nodded at two burly twenty-something guys in dark suits who sat at the next table.

The guy that faced me had a shaved head that glistened with sweat, despite the casino's blasting a/c. He seemed to be the more senior of the two men. He nodded at Rocco as I sat down.

I hadn't noticed the men before, but they were clearly Rocco's bodyguards.

They had apparently noticed me, judging from the way they eyed me up and down.

I scowled at them and sat down across from Rocco. "I'm so sorry to hear about your grandma, Rocco."

I was a little short on the details from Aunt Pearl, so I didn't know what else to say. "What happened, exactly?"

"She got hit." Rocco's voice was flat, and he was surprisingly calm considering his grandmother had been murdered.

"She was hit by a car?" I flashed back to Tyler's comments.

Maybe it was another accident that wasn't so accidental after all. I still couldn't believe that someone might have killed Carla, despite what Aunt Pearl claimed.

He shook his head. "Not literally."

"Uh...how exactly did she die?" I sipped my beer and steeled myself for the grisly details. I felt terrible asking at a time like this, but I had to know if Aunt Pearl's account was true.

"I found her in the lap pool, floating face up. At first, I just thought she was floating with her eyes closed. But she never woke up." Rocco's voice broke. "The police said it was an accident—that she drowned."

"But you said someone…"

He nodded. "Somebody took her out. I'm sure of it. I just don't know how to prove it."

I shuddered. I had covered a few accidental drownings for the Westwick Corners Weekly. I couldn't put my finger on it, but something didn't add up. "How soon after did you find her?"

"We had eaten lunch together less than an hour before that. I only came back to her place because I had forgotten my wallet."

"You were the last person to see her alive?"

He nodded. "I was suspicious as soon as I saw her in the pool. She never ever even went within ten feet of that pool. She was deathly afraid of water."

Since I was stuck here in town until after the funeral, it wouldn't hurt to do a little sleuthing. "Did the medical examiner do an autopsy yet?"

"No. I don't think they will either. Word is that they consider it an accident."

I was surprised that they wouldn't do at least a cursory investigation, considering the Racatelli name. A crime boss's accidental drowning should raise all sorts of red flags. "Maybe the medical examiner will do an autopsy anyway. Despite what the police say."

I could think of only one reason for the police to conclude it was an accident without any sort of investigation.

A cover-up.

I refocused on Rocco, trying to make sense of it all.

Rocco wrung one hand inside the other. "I really need your talents to get to the bottom of this, Cen."

"Why me? I wouldn't know the first thing about how to help. I don't see how—" We didn't exactly advertise our supernatural abilities but as a long-time Westwick Corners resident, Rocco was well aware of at least some of the West family talents.

"Pearl already gave me her word. She said you were a bit rusty and all, but that she'd give you a hand."

"She did?" I was furious at Aunt Pearl's constant pushing, though I felt bad for Rocco. Strangely enough, my preoccupation with returning home had been replaced by sympathy for Rocco. I wanted to do whatever I could to avenge his grandmother's death. But everything about our encounter struck me as a little strange. Rocco acted surprised to see me, yet he and Aunt Pearl had already been talking about me. Maybe it had all been an act.

Rocco nodded. "Whoever did this is gonna pay. Everybody wants our business because Grandma built such a lucrative empire. Bones Battilana is no exception. He wants a piece of the action without doing any of the work."

The larger of the two wise guys at the next table swore and punched his fist into the table at the mention of Carla's husband, now a widower.

"They ain't getting in on the action, not if I can help it." Rocco frowned. "But first, I've got to stop them. That's where you come in."

"Oh?" If Rocco's suspicions were founded, he really should be talking to the police, not an incompetent witch. "Have you raised your suspicions with the police?"

"I didn't push it. They wouldn't have done much anyway.

They're happy if we knock each other off. That makes less work for them. As far as they're concerned, these turf wars are just a cost of doing business. Grandma built a very successful money laundering operation. She runs—I mean ran—everything through this casino. Battilana's boys have threatened me, telling me I'm next. Once I'm gone, the business is theirs."

While I felt sorry for Rocco, I wasn't about to join forces with a crime syndicate.

I covered my ears. "Why are you telling me all this? The more I know, the more I'm in danger too." Now I was doubly mad at Aunt Pearl. The free hotel suite pretty much obligated us to help Rocco out.

"I'm now the sole Racatelli survivor, so the business falls to me. That means that I'm next on the hit list." Rocco frowned and thought for a moment. "Don't worry though. Since you're not in the business, you'll be left alone."

"What makes you so sure about that?" My pulse quickened as I leaned across the table. Getting involved was a bad idea. My heart said yes, even if my brain said no. In the end, my emotions won out. I wanted to help him.

"It's an unwritten rule. Now that you know, we've got no time to waste. Let me tell you about Grandma." Rocco signaled the waiter for another round and leaned forward.

As a journalist, part of me was dying to know the behind-the-scenes story. The risk-averse side of me wanted to remain in the dark. I downed the remaining liquid in my beer mug. "I'm listening."

CHAPTER 13

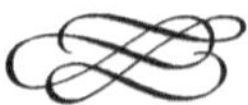

"You know I'd do anything for you. Just tell me what you need." I leaned forward across the table and stared into Rocco Racatelli's beautiful blues. Maybe Aunt Pearl was right after all. We both had family secrets, so it seemed like a natural partnership. We were destined to be together.

"I'm so glad you and your family came out for the funeral." Rocco patted my hand. "I'm still in shock over what's happened, but this morning was a close call. I came pretty close to getting crossed off Bones Battilana's hit list."

"The guys in the lobby this morning?"

Rocco nodded. "He plans to kill me and scare away the customers at the same time. Then he'll be free to muscle in on the Racatelli business without anyone getting in his way. Either I get him, or he gets me."

"Maybe there's another way to handle it. We could cast a spell to immobilize him or something." I was uncertain about Aunt Pearl's plans, except that they almost certainly included witchcraft. Now her bad idea sounded good. A spell avoided the likelihood of violence.

"Even if it worked, how long would it last?" Rocco glanced sideways at his burly bodyguards, who seemed more absorbed by the menu than any potential danger. I wondered if they were the same men who had protected Carla. If so, their inattention was definitely part of the problem.

"I think we can find a permanent solution." I was anything but certain, but something inside of me just wanted to say whatever would make Rocco feel better.

The server approached our table with drinks. She was a wisp of a girl who looked barely out of high school. Her tray hand shook visibly as she placed our drinks on the table.

Rocco smiled and waited for her to leave. Once she was out of earshot he leaned across the table and spoke in a low voice. "You sure about this, Cen? It could be dangerous."

"As long as you've got our backs while we get everything in place, it should be fine. We'll take care of Bones so you can get back to taking care of business." I squeezed his hand. The element of danger just seemed to strengthen my feelings for him. Rocco was a known quantity, and we could build a comfortable life together. So what if he had an unconventional job? I was pretty unconventional too.

I was a witch, after all.

Maybe I should just forget about Tyler. As Westwick Corners' sheriff, he followed rules and regulations. My family broke them. He represented order, and we were chaos. I would just create trouble for him.

Rocco, on the other hand, was an outcast just like me. We shared common ground, and nothing my family did could ever hurt his reputation.

He patted my hand and smiled.

I smiled back.

I jumped as something crashed across the bar. The crash was followed by breaking glass. I turned towards the noise just in time to see the server collapsed in a heap beside the bar. She had collided with another server, who fell into the obese bartender behind the bar. He hit the glass shelves behind him, and the whole thing toppled like dominoes.

"What the—" Rocco jumped to his feet. He looked uncertain of whether to help and potentially attract attention, or make himself scarce.

"Something just happened." My hand flew to my chest.

"No kidding."

"No, I mean something just happened to me." The loud noise had jolted me to awareness.

I eyed Rocco, who suddenly wasn't so attractive anymore. He just looked like a larger grown-up version of my high school schoolmate. His muscled torso had morphed into a stocky man with a slight beer belly.

I blurted it out before thinking. "I think Aunt Pearl put an attraction spell on us."

"What are you talking about?"

"This thing that we're feeling for each other, it's not real. The spell was broken by that loud crash." The spell had a safety mechanism to ensure that those under its power were released in potentially dangerous situations. The loud crash had restored our senses, or at least mine.

Rocco frowned. "Of course it's real." A look of uncertainty flashed across his face. "You're telling me you're faking your feelings for me?"

"No—I mean, it wasn't really my feelings in the first place. I like you, Rocco. Just not in that way." I realized in shock that I had essentially agreed to a supernatural hit while under the influence of Aunt Pearl's spell. All I wanted to do right now was confront her and give her a piece of my mind.

But I had given Rocco my word.

A promise I couldn't keep.

Rocco looked hurt. He turned away, confused.

"It's just me, Rocco. Can't you feel the difference between your thoughts for me a moment ago and now?"

He shook his head. "I still want to take you—" He frowned. "That's weird. I forgot what I was going to say."

"The spell's worn off. I'm sorry, but I can't get involved in your criminal activities. We'll get Carla's killer all right, but it won't be with witchcraft." I was already fuzzy on what I had actually promised, but maybe Rocco was too.

"You've got to help me, Cen. Bones' thugs are tailing me, just waiting for the chance to knock me off."

"I'm sure we can place a protection spell on you. I'll talk to Aunt Pearl." One thing still puzzled me. "You inherit Carla's estate, but what happens if you die? Who's next in line?"

Rocco paused. "Her husband."

My mouth dropped open.

"Bones Battilana."

"Are you sure?"

Rocco gave me a confused stare.

"What I mean is—isn't he already first in line? The husband comes before a child or a grandchild, no matter how recent the marriage. If that's the case, he doesn't have any reason to kill you. He's already going to inherit everything."

Rocco's shocked expression told me I was right. Something else was going on, and I intended to find out what.

I was also furious at my aunt. Because of her spell, I had essentially promised to knock off a mobster. It was dangerous, illegal, and life shortening.

But a promise was a promise, and I always kept my word.

I just had to find another way to do it.

CHAPTER 14

Rocco's fortunes had changed dramatically in the ten years since I had last seen him. Maybe his character had too.

I refocused on Rocco's story. I was still amazed at the Racatellis' vast real estate holdings, of which the Hotel Babylon was apparently just a small part. The family holdings had to be worth hundreds of millions of dollars.

I cut to the chase. "How exactly does the Racatelli business earn a living?"

"If I told you I'd have to kill you." Rocco smiled for the first time. "Seriously, though, you don't need to worry about any of that."

"I'm not kidding, Rocco. I can't help you unless you tell me everything." As I leaned forward, I realized that I was functioning exactly as Aunt Pearl had intended. I had fallen into her trap, hook, line, and sinker.

Rocco sipped his drink. "Grandma edged out the competition. Not with fear or violence, but by paying higher wages and bonuses. The employees were very loyal to her. It's not that she won the best properties. She didn't. Instead, she took lousy properties and made them into winners with lots of hard work. Bones didn't like that. He wanted the best for himself. But it wasn't just that. Bones didn't like being bested by Carla."

"Because she's a woman?"

Rocco shrugged. "I think so. It got worse once she became his wife. I don't know. Grandma told me it was just a marriage of convenience for her, but I guess Bones saw things differently."

My mouth dropped open. "She was using him?"

"Why not? He was using her, too. They both wanted something from their 'arrangement'." Rocco made quote marks with his fingers. "Grandma just wanted something casual."

It never occurred to me that gray-haired seniors like Carla or Aunt Pearl had flings, or got married to people they weren't in love with. "You make it sound so sordid."

"You sound like a seventy-year-old. You need a little Las Vegas to loosen you up."

I glared at Rocco, angry that he made such snap judgments about me. "I'm fine the way I am, thank you."

"Grandma was just a bit of a free spirit. She really just wanted a hook-up. Bones is the one that insisted on marriage."

I gasped. That certainly wasn't the Carla I remembered, but then again, I hadn't seen her since I was a teenager.

"But she did end up marrying him. Why the sudden change?" Spouses or significant others were usually suspect number one, but the couples involved were usually much younger.

"Grandma thought it would stop the violence from escalating. Give him what he wanted. At least, let him think that. She made him sign a pre-nup, though. She worried that Bones was only marrying her to wrest control of our holdings."

"Like this hotel?" Lots of people probably wanted to hone in on the Racatelli racket. I was surprised that Bones had still gone ahead with the wedding if there was a pre-nup. On the other hand, I didn't know all the legal details. Maybe Bones still stood to gain something, even with the pre-nup. It seemed that Rocco benefited from Carla's death more than anyone. If he could hold onto it, that is.

Rocco nodded, his eyes moist with tears. "That, and a few other things. Grandma later got cold feet and tried to back out of the wedding, but Bones threatened her. So she went through with it. But she left everything to me."

"That hardly sounds like true love to me." I suddenly felt very sorry for Rocco. Criminal or not, he just had his whole family stolen from him. Pre-nup or not, Bones had obviously been after something other than Carla's affections.

"Where is Bones? Have you seen him?"

"I avoid him whenever possible," Rocco said. "He'll be at the funeral of course—playing the grieving husband."

"That's awkward."

Rocco nodded slowly. "Whoever did this is gonna pay. But that will have to wait till after the funeral."

A waiter brought martinis for Rocco, me, and the two tough guys at the next table, though we hadn't ordered anything. The last thing I needed or wanted was more alcohol.

Rocco reached across the table and touched my hand. "About the funeral—I'll see you there tomorrow?"

I nodded, not knowing what else to say. Despite the organized crime rumors that had always surrounded the family, I never suspected that Carla had any involvement. Now my interest was piqued. I wanted to bolt from my seat and sprint upstairs to find everything I could about the Racatelli family, their secret lives, and untimely deaths.

The funeral had taken on a new meaning for me, and I wanted to do whatever I could to help Rocco. Whatever his job now, he was still the same boy I had grown up with. Even criminals loved their grandmas, and no one deserved to be taken out by a cold-blooded killer. Besides, I had never been to a mob funeral.

I flashed back to Tyler's warning. As long as I was careful, everything would be fine.

I smiled at Rocco as I sipped my drink. "I'll be there."

"All's fair in love and war," Aunt Pearl said. "But we can probably boost Rocco's odds a little."

I had returned to the suite to find Mom passed out, Christophe cooking something in the kitchen, and Aunt Pearl staring intently at the TV. It was some sort of championship poker tournament.

I crossed my arms and stood in front of the television, blocking her view. "You're wasting your time with your crazy spells. Whatever you did to Rocco and me is undone now."

"Whatever are you talking about? I never did a thing." Aunt Pearl waved her hand in dismissal. "Now get out of the way so I don't miss any of the action. I think somebody's about to go all in and blow it."

I turned and faced the screen. Three men and a woman stared intently at their cards. It was duller than a slow motion replay of a golf tournament. I grabbed the remote and shut the TV off.

"Hey! I was watching that." Aunt Pearl tried to grab the remote from me, but I held it just out of reach.

"It's one thing to kidnap me, but putting me under a spell and putting my life in danger? That's not okay, Aunt Pearl. Luckily the spell broke." If I was in the middle of a turf war, I at least wanted my wits about me.

"You used your undo spell? Nice work!" She immediately brightened. "See, all you had to do was apply yourself."

"I didn't do anything. The spell wore off by itself because it wasn't strong enough. In any event, I won't stand for your matchmaking and meddling." I placed the remote on the coffee table.

Aunt Pearl stuck out her lower lip in a pout. "I was only trying to help, Cen. You've been so grumpy since you canceled your wedding that I thought I could spice up your life a bit. You don't have to be so ungrateful about it."

Just like Aunt Pearl to remind me of my almost-wedding to Brayden Banks, who had sold me down the river to line his own pockets. Money seemed to be at the root of all evil in the world. Carla's wealth had also been her downfall.

"I am not ungrateful, and I have enough spice—" I had said too much.

Aunt Pearl rolled her eyes as she grabbed the remote and turned the TV back on. "Could have fooled me."

"You never should have placed that spell on Rocco and me. Now I've promised him something I can't deliver." I told her about Rocco's mistaken belief that he was Carla's heir. "He knows about the marriage, of course, but he said that Bones signed a pre-nup."

Aunt Pearl laughed. "Bones would never sign anything like that. But it's not really a big deal. We'll figure something out."

"But how—Rocco's about to lose his livelihood. And Bones has just gained a whole new business empire." I recounted Rocco's version of Carla's romance—if you could call it that—and the forced marriage. "Rocco told me that the police are treating Carla's death as an accident."

"That's not possible," Aunt Pearl said.

"What about Bones? Do you think he killed her?"

"What about him?" Aunt Pearl's face darkened. "Never mind. We'll talk about that later."

Something in my aunt's voice told me not to press further, but I did anyway. "Carla must've had tons of enemies, considering her line of work. Even Rocco had a motive."

"Not Rocco." Aunt Pearl shook her head. "Rocco loved his grandma. You're right about other people wanting her dead, though. I just wish we had gotten here sooner. When things started escalating, she begged me for help. But I was too late." A solitary tear ran down her cheek.

I plopped down beside my aunt on the sofa and squeezed her shoulders. Aunt Pearl had always been a pillar of strength to me, despite her small stature. Now she just seemed tiny and vulnerable.

"Please tell me that you're not a mobster too." I felt like I didn't really even know my aunt anymore, and I couldn't handle any more secrets. Especially anything that involved trigger-happy gangsters. We were way too involved in other people's business. Ruthless people, who would stop at nothing to get rid of us if we got in the way.

She pulled away. "Of course I'm not. But I am a friend of Carla's. With or without you, I'll do anything protect Rocco. And avenge Carla's death. Now, are you in or not?"

"Of course I'm in." I sighed. Aunt Pearl had strung me along like a violin, and I had no choice but to play.

CHAPTER 16

It couldn't have been a hotter day for a funeral. We stood on the asphalt driveway, a few feet away from the massive Racatelli mausoleum that dwarfed the other cemetery plots. A dozen or so guests stood in somber silence as we waited for the funeral to get underway.

I turned to Aunt Pearl. "Will Bones be at the funeral? I don't see him."

She shrugged. "Who knows?"

He certainly had a motive to kill Carla, even with the pre-nup in place. With Carla gone, he had one less competitor. Even so, I couldn't imagine that Carla's own husband would miss the funeral, but Bones was nowhere to be seen.

Maybe he was already on the run, despite the police claim that Carla's death was an accident. Or maybe he was already dipping his toes into the Racatelli empire waters while Rocco's attention was focused on the funeral.

"Tell me when you see him," I said.

Aunt Pearl stood beside me, but she might as well have been a million miles away. Maybe it was the hot sun, or maybe she was pre-occupied with memories of Carla. I tapped her arm.

"Huh?"

"When you see Bones, point him out to me, okay?" The funeral procession was behind schedule, and I was roasting in the hundred-degree heat. The black woolen dress Aunt Pearl had conjured up for me was heavy and unbreathable. My legs were imprisoned in heavy black stockings and too-small pumps, also courtesy of Aunt Pearl. As usual, her wardrobe choices were meant to simultaneously punish and incentivize me to improve my own witchcraft skills. In typical Aunt Pearl fashion, the medium was the message. Her wardrobe choice of wool in the desert was designed to make me feel the heat.

"Keep your voice down, Cendrine." Aunt Pearl's eyes narrowed. "Don't say his name or you'll attract too much attention."

The gravity of the situation suddenly hit me. I was at a real-life mob funeral. But maybe my excitement at experiencing a real-life Sopranos was misplaced. We could easily get caught in the crossfire of Mafia family warfare.

"Maybe we shouldn't have come to the funeral after all," I said. "What if something happens?" The more I thought about it, the less sense it made for any of us to attend a funeral and be surrounded by known criminals. "What if those wise guys from the lobby come to pay their respects?"

Aunt Pearl shrugged. "All the more reason for us to attend. Rocco needs more than bodyguards. He needs a shield of magic if he's going to survive the day."

She squeezed my arm in reassurance. "Everything will be fine, Cen. Just relax. We have to be here. Carla was practically family."

I turned to Mom, who looked cool and elegant in a sleeveless black linen dress that ended just below her knees. It was simple, elegant, and far better suited to the Las Vegas climate than my woolen number. "I barely knew Carla Racatelli when she lived in

Westwick Corners. She didn't miss me when she moved away ten years ago. She certainly won't notice me missing from her funeral."

"Maybe not, but your presence will make a big difference to Rocco, knowing he has your support." Mom patted my hand.

Rocco. I had promised I would be at the funeral, but he had so much else on his mind that he'd probably already forgotten about me. If Aunt Pearl's spell was broken for me, surely it was for him too. In some weird way, that disappointed me.

"Why does Rocco even need my support? I haven't seen or talked to him in years."

My pulse quickened as I remembered his hand on mine. I was strangely attracted to him on a physical level, though my brain told me he was all wrong for me. Maybe the spell wasn't completely gone after all.

I wanted Tyler, not Rocco, but that wasn't happening until I left Las Vegas. I flashed back to Tyler when he pulled us over on the highway. His brilliant smile, looking handsome in his uniform.

It suddenly dawned on me that Aunt Pearl probably had an inkling of my secret attraction to Tyler. Maybe she had kidnapped me not just to help Rocco, but to keep me from Tyler. As sheriff, he was the bane of her existence. She was forever testing the limits of the law and getting into trouble. She would be horrified at the thought of me dating him. But we had gone to great lengths to keep our secret from everyone including Aunt Pearl, so it was possible that she didn't know a thing.

Or maybe she knew everything. I shivered.

"Oh, Cen?"

"Yes?"

"Did I mention that you're a pallbearer? Better take your place behind Rocco." She pointed towards Rocco, who stood with four elderly men. I wondered if they were Racatelli relatives, roped into action. If they were, they looked a lot older than Carla had been.

"What? No!" Suddenly everyone went silent and all eyes were on me. Even the traffic on the nearby street seemed to have come to a standstill.

"Cendrine West, get your butt in gear and get in line." Aunt Pearl shooed me towards the men. For the first time, I noticed the coffin on a stand behind them.

And everyone noticed me. I slinked over towards the men and, since I had no choice, took my place.

I jumped at a low whistle.

"Psst!" Aunt Pearl gave me a thumbs up.

That attracted the attention of two swarthy-looking men built like NFL linebackers. I recognized them immediately as Rocco's security guys and wondered why I was a pallbearer instead of one or both of the two muscle men.

Of course.

They needed to keep their hands free, in case they had to pull their guns to protect Rocco.

I shuddered. Anyone shooting at Rocco would be aiming towards me too. I would be standing a few feet directly behind him as pallbearer.

This was too much to ask of anyone, and I wasn't willing to put my life in mortal danger by carrying a crime boss's coffin. I walked towards Aunt Pearl. Her back was turned as she talked with Mom, so she didn't see me until I tapped her elbow.

"Cendrine West, get back in your place." Aunt Pearl's eyes widened. "Hurry!"

I shook my head. "No, Aunt Pearl. I don't belong here, and I want to go home." With no car and with no money for a plane ticket, my options were limited. I looked helplessly at Mom. Couldn't she do something?

Mom shook her head ever so slightly, hoping her sister wouldn't notice.

"No, you have to stay, Cen." Aunt Pearl pursed her lips. "The procession needs you as pallbearer. I desperately need your help too."

"Why me?" I felt guilty making waves at such a solemn occasion, but I also felt trouble brewing. Whatever Aunt Pearl had up her sleeve was bound to be dangerous, embarrassing, or both.

"You're a distraction." She tucked a wayward lock of hair behind my ear. "You know, eye candy. To hold the attention of those trigger-happy young guns while Ruby and I work our magic."

"I don't see why—"

"Don't argue with me. Remember, I sprained my ankle, so you're taking my place as pallbearer." Aunt Pearl's bottom lip stuck out in an exaggerated pout as a walker magically appeared in front of her. "That's the story. I'll make it up to you, I promise."

I frowned. "I don't remember you hurting yourself. You looked pretty spry earlier today."

"That was just an act, Cen. Look at me, I can barely walk." Aunt Pearl's bottom lip quivered. "If you don't take my place you'll ruin Carla's funeral."

"I doubt she will notice."

"Just help me out of this jam," Aunt Pearl said. "You only have to walk a few feet and it will be over."

Arguing with Aunt Pearl was futile. She always won an argument, and I was too tired to put up much of a fight.

The other pallbearers stared pointedly at me. Apparently, I was holding up the show.

I didn't know what was more horrifying—carrying a corpse at a mob funeral, or my seemingly uncontrollable attraction to Rocco. What I did know was that Aunt Pearl would make waves if I didn't follow her wishes.

The last thing I wanted was closer ties with someone who operated on the fringes of society. Because if there was one thing I knew about the Racatelli family, it was that they were connected to some very powerful people in the crime world. People I didn't want to know that I even existed.

More troubling was Aunt Pearl's apparent tie to the Racatelli family. She hadn't mentioned Carla even once since the Racatelli family's sudden move from Westwick Corners over a decade ago, and she wasn't one for long distance communications. Something else was up, I felt sure of it.

CHAPTER 17

The funeral finally got underway an hour late, with no explanation given for the delay. While Rocco and his entourage waited in his air-conditioned limo, Aunt Pearl, Mom, and I stood on the hot asphalt with the rest of the mourners, waiting for the ceremony to begin. The afternoon sun beat down mercilessly, and I already felt sunburnt. I wiped sweat from my brow and shifted my weight from one uncomfortable shoe to another.

Rocco stepped out of his limo, flanked by four beefy bodyguards. Two I recognized from earlier, and two I hadn't seen before. We waited as Rocco and his entourage walked slowly up the asphalt road to where we stood outside the building.

It was a day meant more for tank tops and shorts than winter-weight wool suits, and I felt faint from the heat. I couldn't wait until the service was over.

The undertaker slid the coffin from the hearse and directed the pallbearers to our places. Rather than being behind Rocco as planned, I was sandwiched between two frail-looking men in their seventies. Both had hunched backs and looked even more ready to collapse from the heat than I was.

I had never been a pallbearer before and was extremely nervous. It wasn't really the kind of thing you could do a dry run on. Luckily I had one of the middle spots, so I would simply take cues from the other pallbearers. They were all decades older than me, so I assumed that they had probably done this sort of thing before.

I took my place and grasped the metal handhold. The casket was on my right. I had no confidence whatsoever in any of my fellow pallbearers, who all looked like they'd have trouble carrying a bag of groceries further than a city block. I just hoped we were collectively strong enough. The distance to the gravesite was only fifty yards, but plenty could go wrong.

It seemed strange that I was the only female pallbearer, particularly as I was a last minute substitute for Aunt Pearl. She was a shade under five feet tall and there was no way she could have pulled it off without resorting to witchcraft. She was an odd choice to begin with. We all were, considering all the young, sturdy-looking men around. There were probably a hundred people present, any one of which were probably closer to Carla or Rocco than I was. I could see why the bodyguards were given a pass, but what about the other able-bodied guests? Why weren't they chosen as pallbearers?

I wiped sweat from my brow with my free hand as I realized Aunt Pearl had planned my pallbearer duties all along. As usual, she had a plan. I just wished I knew what it was.

I grew more exhausted with each step. I struggled to keep Carla's coffin level with the other pallbearers who, though frail, were quite a bit taller than I was. I held my arms uncomfortably high just to keep in alignment with the others.

Carla's coffin was heavy beyond belief, and I felt as though I would collapse at any moment. Judging by our slow gait, the other pallbearers had problems balancing the weight too.

We continued our glacial pace over the uneven asphalt. I counted every step as we lurched and then steadied ourselves, over and over again. We trudged towards the burial site, still a good forty yards away. I grew hotter and sweatier as the coffin's sharp metal handle dug into my hand. We were about halfway there, but the pain in my hand had become unbearable.

At this rate, I might pass out before we reached the gravesite. I glanced at my frail, elderly male companions and wondered about our ability to pull this thing off.

One, two, three…

I silently counted my steps, thinking I had a hundred at the most before I could put the heavy wooden box down.

Fourteen, fifteen…

The man in front of me tripped over a crack in the asphalt and lurched forwards and sideways. He fell to his knees, still grasping the casket with one hand.

My knees strained under the weight, and it was all I could do not to trip on top of him. I instantly regretted my lapsed weightlifting workouts. My right leg buckled as I lunged forward. That put me out of sync with my fellow pallbearers and their shuffling pace. I teetered for a moment and then regained my balance. We all paused for a moment as the coffin's weight shifted precariously.

Someone helped the fallen man back to his feet. To my surprise, he resumed his place in front of me. I had expected someone to take his place, but no one did.

"Wow, this is heavy," I said under my breath. "Carla must have gained a lot of weight." If any of the other pallbearers heard me, they didn't acknowledge it.

"Ready? One, two, three." The man in front spoke just loud enough for me to hear. "Let's go slower this time."

I groaned. If anything, I thought we should speed up before we lost momentum. I didn't dare say anything, though.

We obeyed and shuffled down the asphalt towards the undertaker like a geriatric military column in slow motion. The undertaker directed us to turn right off the asphalt and onto the grass. We trudged along the uneven ground down a row of gravestones. It was becoming harder and harder to stay in formation, maintain my balance and hold the casket level all at the same time.

I focused on my footsteps, putting one foot in front of the other.

We managed a few more feet onto the grass when my balance shifted. The casket handle dug even further into my hand, cutting off all circulation. My hand went numb and I could no longer feel the casket's metal handle. I willed myself to go forward. Just a few more steps and I would be done.

It had been a long time since I last saw Carla Racatelli, but even allowing for ten years of Las Vegas-sized meal portions, the casket was heavy beyond belief.

Which seemed odd, because the Carla I remembered was a lightweight like Aunt Pearl who barely weighed a hundred pounds. Any weight gain would be dispersed amongst all six of us, so it shouldn't require superhuman strength. Once again my knees buckled under the weight.

My hand throbbed in pain as I focused on the ground, counting the last few steps and the seconds until we reached Carla's final resting place where I could finally release my aching hand.

A small group of men and women dressed in dark clothing gathered around the open gravesite, with the rest of the procession following behind us. We gained momentum as we grew closer.

Less than ten feet until I could release my hand.

The next few moments were a blur as the casket bottom cracked and something broke through. I froze in my tracks as the weight shifted.

A woman screamed and pointed in our direction.

I glanced at the casket and my mouth dropped open in horror.

A set of legs protruded from the bottom of the casket right beside me.

I screamed.

Hairy legs. Definitely male calves protruding from pushed up trouser legs. The legs were attached to a body that was undeniably male, with a potbelly barely constrained under a black pinstriped suit.

Not Carla.

The corpse thudded on the ground like a crash test dummy afflicted with advanced rigor mortis.

The coffin lurched skyward from the sudden decrease in weight. I tried to right myself. This time it was too little, too late. The coffin flew from our hands as it dropped forward headfirst onto the grass and tilted sideways. It landed with a thud on top of the corpse.

Mom screamed and pointed to the casket. "That's not Carla."

It sure wasn't, unless Carla Racatelli had turned into an overweight man.

Aunt Pearl swooned and fell backwards into the crowd of people huddled around the coffin. Two burly thirty-something men in black suits caught her and helped her to the back of the hearse, where she rested against the tailgate.

A hinge squeaked as the casket cover swung open. Tiny Carla Racatelli smiled serenely at the crowd, her arms folded neatly across her rigid body. She had somehow remained inside the casket, and for that I was grateful.

A couple of teenage boys snapped pictures with their cell phones. I shuddered to think of what they would be posting on Facebook, Instagram, or some other social media site. It had taken death, but Carla and her uninvited guest were about to go viral.

"Hey, put your phones away and help us right the casket!" I pointed at the boys and directed them to pick up the casket and carry it to the gravesite.

They were so shocked at my outburst that they reluctantly slipped their phones into their pockets and complied.

"Serves her right," muttered a hunchbacked man dressed all in black. "She got what was coming to her."

An argument broke out between two men standing behind

him, while still others speculated on who would be hit next. The somber funeral had turned into an Italian shouting match, and I wondered when they would start throwing things at each other.

Or worse, I thought as I spotted Rocco's bodyguards all reaching under their suit jackets.

"What the hell is going on?" Rocco Racatelli stepped in front of the mortician, blocking his path. "What have you done to my grandma?"

"I—I don't understand. I put Mrs. Racatelli in the coffin myself." The mortician flushed and broke into a sweat as he knelt on the grass. He took a deep breath and closed the casket lid. "All good. She's still in there."

"My grandma prepaid for a funeral with all the works," Rocco said. "Not some two-for-one Groupon deal with a half-assed casket. You're going to regret this."

The two men who had helped Aunt Pearl suddenly stepped closer to the mortician. He trembled, visibly afraid.

"Not now, boys." Rocco waved them away.

Aunt Pearl suddenly materialized at my side. "Carla would be mortified. She never flew economy class. She would never do something cheap like a shared coffin."

The mortician paled. "Someone has tampered with the coffin. It's got a false bottom."

"You mean like a double-decker coffin?" That explained the heavy casket. Together, Carla and the mystery man probably weighed over three hundred pounds.

It was certainly an ingenious way to get rid of a body, and it had only worked because of Carla's tiny stature.

At least, it had almost worked.

Carla's body was on top, so if not for the coffin fiasco, no one would have known that two bodies shared the casket. Rarely did anyone search for missing persons in a graveyard.

But just who was the unidentified corpse? Someone had to be missing him. "Anyone know who this guy is?"

Everyone stared at me like I was an idiot.

"You don't know?" Rocco hesitated before answering. "Danny 'Bones' Battilana."

"Bones?" I gasped. This pot-bellied man looked nothing like his nickname, and I couldn't believe he was the one who had broken Mom's heart. I stole a glance at Mom, who sniffled into a Kleenex.

"Oh. I just assumed you knew him." Rocco's brows arched in surprise.

I shook my head, a bit miffed that I was apparently the only one who didn't know of Mom's secret affair. "I've uh, heard of him."

Death gave Bones an ironclad alibi. Judging by the condition of his corpse, he had been dead longer than Carla. The bullet hole in the middle of his forehead also implied that his death wasn't from natural causes.

If Bones didn't kill Carla, then who did? Maybe the same person had killed both of them. They were both the heads of their respective crime families, so clearly someone was vying for power.

I scanned the crowd, suddenly feeling vulnerable. Whoever the killer was, he or she was probably here at the graveside. I stepped away from Rocco, just in case he was the next target.

I jumped as someone touched my elbow. I yanked it away. "What the—"

"Cen, stop acting so jumpy." Mom clutched my arm. Tears streamed down her face, and she was clearly distraught. She leaned against me. "Who would do something like this?"

Should I pretend not to know about Bones? I looked to Aunt Pearl for guidance but she was too busy talking to Rocco to notice. I decided now wasn't the time or place to question her about her secret lover. "Somebody wanting to cover up a murder, I guess."

"Why hide him in Carla's casket, of all places?" Mom's brows furrowed together. "They look like they're sleeping together."

"I'm sorry." It wasn't my place to tell her, but Mom had no idea how right she was. I hoped nobody would, just to spare her the hurt. "You seem to be handling it okay."

"Huh? Well, these things happen." Mom shrugged. "Not much we can do about it."

I was dying to get the lowdown on Mom's relationship with Bones Battilana, but I didn't dare ask, in case someone overheard. Whoever knew of Mom's relationship with Bones might come after her, assuming she was privy to his secrets. It didn't take a genius to figure out that a tit-for-tat mob vendetta would only escalate things. I had to figure out a way to stop the turf war before it claimed more victims.

CHAPTER 18

Rocco had spared no expense for Carla's funeral. There was enough gourmet food to feed an army of mourners, and mobster mourners seemed to have especially hearty appetites. A steady stream of guests trickled in and out of the banquet room to pay their respects to Rocco. He stood by the doors, chatting with three women who looked to be about Carla's age.

Another dozen or so people milled around a large buffet table laden with canapés, fancy finger sandwiches, French pastries, and exotic fruits. But most of the crowd gathered at the bar, where a bartender poured liberal shots of whiskey, brandy, and Italian liqueurs. The conversations grew louder with each pour, most focussed on the Bones Battilana coffin fiasco, and speculation on how exactly he came to his dramatic end.

It was hard to ignore a bullet in the forehead.

I stood in a corner of the room, trying unsuccessfully to blend into the charcoal-colored drapes that framed the large windows. Beyond was an unobstructed view of the cemetery and the roped-off gravesite crime scene, where the police busily collected evidence.

Strangely enough, the police remained outside. No one came inside to question us. I got the feeling that the police already had a short list of suspects, most of whom were probably already right here in this room. No one inside seemed to take notice of the activities outside, however. The mourners seemed, for the most part, unconcerned.

I was still shaken that I had dropped the casket. It was embarrassing to be the weakest link amongst all the pallbearers, who were all at least forty years older than me. I vowed to restart my fitness routine as soon as I got home.

But my slip-up had a plus side. If it hadn't been for me, 'Bones' Battilana would have remained suspect number one in Carla's murder, sending the investigation off in the wrong direction. Now that he was off the suspect list, we could focus on other leads, instead of assuming that Danny Battilana was guilty and on the run. I felt like an unsung heroine of sorts, having "discovered" the body. Strangely, no one else seemed to share my sentiments.

I felt terrible for Mom. It was one thing to discover a dead boyfriend, but to have him drop out of a coffin was something else entirely. Mom had handled herself exceptionally well with poise and dignity. At the moment she stood beside me, halfway through her second helping of tiramisu.

"Are you sure you're okay?" I studied her closely.

"Why wouldn't I be?" Mom dabbed her lips with a napkin. "Free trip to Vegas, great food, and an incredible penthouse to stay in. What more could I ask for?"

"You know what I mean. Bones."

"What about him?" Mom's brows furrowed together.

"He was your…uh, friend, right? Aren't you the least bit upset?"

"What? I barely knew him, but I could never figure out what Pearl saw in him. She was in love with him."

CHAPTER 19

Mom and I stood at one end of the bar, which gave us a clear vantage point of the room as well as the police work underway outside. Other than several uniformed police officers guarding the scene, nothing much seemed to be happening.

I turned to Mom. "Just how many women was Bones dating? There's Carla, Aunt Pearl, and you." I counted on my fingers. "Am I missing anyone?"

"No, Cen. Like I told you, I never dated Bones," Mom said. "Couldn't even stand the sight of him. But Pearl and Carla were both crazy for him. That probably ruined their friendship. Bones left Pearl for Carla, and then they wanted to kill each other. That guy's not worth it, if you ask me."

My mouth dropped open. "But Aunt Pearl said—"

Mom dismissed me with a wave of her hand. "You know how she is. Never a straight answer, and she constantly makes stuff up. She likes to stir up controversy."

Aunt Pearl had not only stayed silent on her romantic rivalry with Carla, but she had apparently lied to me about Mom's relationship with Bones too. I believed Mom over Aunt Pearl, so I was relieved by her denial.

But Mom's claim presented a problem. It meant Aunt Pearl had motives to kill both Carla and Bones. I knew she didn't have it in her, but no one else would believe that about my cantankerous, fibbing aunt.

I could vouch for Aunt Pearl's whereabouts during our RV trip, but not for any time earlier. The police couldn't ignore the bullet in Bones' forehead, which meant they would be searching for suspects. It was only a matter of time before they focussed their sights on romantic partners like Aunt Pearl.

I turned back to Mom. "You're absolutely sure you didn't date Bones? Not even once?" I wanted to be absolutely sure of the facts.

"Over my dead body! I can't stand that man."

"Sssh. We don't want anyone getting the wrong idea." A few people at the bar glanced in our direction, including Aunt Pearl, who was out of earshot at the opposite end of the bar. She was practically sitting on the lap of a seventyish man. He wore an expensive-looking tailored pink shirt under a black suit with matching pink pinstripes. Apparently, pinstripes were a timeless fashion classic in the mob world. "Who's that man Aunt Pearl is talking to?"

"That's The Man."

"Huh?" She obviously hadn't spent much time mourning Bones.

"Manny 'The Man' La Manna," Mom explained. "Pearl is infatuated with him. I think the feeling's mutual."

I followed her stare to the opposite end of the bar, where the two had intertwined their arms, glasses raised in a toast. "Aunt Pearl has the hots for him too? Since when?"

Mom shrugged. "About a couple of months ago. She's just gone man crazy, Cen. I don't really know what's gotten into her lately. Maybe it's from those weird kale smoothies she drinks."

"I'm going over to see what she's up to." I headed to the center of the bar and caught the attention of the bartender. I first wanted to refill my wine glass with Sauvignon Blanc. Heaven knows I needed fortification to pry the truth out of my aunt. I suspected Aunt Pearl, Mom, or both had lied to me about Bones, and I wasn't letting up until I got to the bottom of it.

Aunt Pearl materialized at my side seconds later. "Don't screw this up with your meddling, Cen. Just mind your business and don't ask questions."

"I thought that's why you brought me here. To meddle." I had plenty of questions that needed answers. In less than twenty-four hours we had been in an RV rollover, involved in a shootout, uncovered a dead man, and were now surrounded by a roomful of America's Most Wanted. "If you won't tell me the truth, maybe somebody else will. Your gentleman friend, for instance. Mr. La Manna."

"You leave Manny out of this."

"But I'm just dying to meet him. I've heard so much about him."

Aunt Pearl's eyes widened in surprise. She glared across the room at Mom and made a hex sign.

Mom just shrugged, though I swore that I saw a trace of a smile on her lips.

"I'll introduce you some other time. I'm in damage control mode right now, trying to keep him from going after Rocco and the Racatelli empire. These merger talks are killing me."

"Manny is a crime boss too?" Aunt Pearl's peacekeeper role surprised me. Diplomacy was hardly her strong suit, and acting as the Henry Kissinger of the mob world seemed both highly dangerous and completely unnecessary. Aside from her complete lack of tact and persuasion, it was very unlikely that any sort of truce would last more than a few hours with these wise guys.

Aunt Pearl nodded. "With both Carla and Bones out of the way, Manny's wasting no time moving in for the kill. He wants Rocco out of the way. He's willing to make a generous offer, but Rocco saying 'no' is not an option."

"I can't believe you are on a first names basis with these people.

You think Manny killed Carla and Bones? Maybe Rocco is next." I sounded just like my aunt, which horrified me.

"That's why we'd better act fast."

"It doesn't look like your shameless flirting is an act at all. You seem to be enjoying yourself."

"Oh, grow up, Cendrine. I'm doing this at great personal sacrifice. It's what's best for all of us."

I closed my hand around her arm. "No, Aunt Pearl. I think we need to mind our own business. Let's go."

To my surprise, Aunt Pearl agreed. "Okay, fine. Let's get out of here."

CHAPTER 20

I scanned the funeral reception for Rocco. I wanted to say goodbye, but without anyone noticing. If Rocco was in danger, I didn't want to be tagged by association.

On second thought, the idea that I could fly under the radar was dumb. I had already attracted the attention of every breathing soul above ground with my attention-getting coffin drop. As a pall-bearer, everyone would assume that I was close to Rocco and the Racatelli family.

Rocco caught my eye and crossed the room. "Recovered from your fall?"

My face flushed. "I'm really sorry about that. It must have been the heat or something. I should probably go back to the hotel and get some rest." I had the perfect excuse to leave. Aside from the Las Vegas heat, my wool suit and geriatric pallbearer partners hadn't done me any favors.

"Not your fault." His intense blue eyes locked on mine.

I nodded towards the bar. "Carla certainly had a lot of friends." The guests seemed more celebratory than somber, but everyone mourned in their own way. Mobsters probably mourned more often than most, so it was understandable for them to act a little jaded.

"Friends?" He chuckled. "More like frenemies—come here to celebrate Grandma's death, and maybe move in on the business. It's a high stakes, ruthless game. People will kill to cut in on the racket. Grandma's killer is amongst us, no doubt."

"Maybe the police will re-open the investigation."

Rocco stared at me in confusion.

"You know, with the casket incident and all. It seems very coincidental for both Carla and Bones to die so suddenly. Maybe someone wanted both of them dead."

Rocco sighed. "Probably at least half the people here. One or more of them knows what happened to Grandma in her swimming pool. She was afraid of water and never went anywhere near that pool. She always kept the pool drained. You've seen how small and shallow that thing is."

I frowned. "No."

"Of course you have, Cen. You're staying in her suite."

"What? Oh yes, of course." I flashed back to the pool, shocked. I was furious at Aunt Pearl for omitting such a major detail. I never dreamt that our suite was the actual site of Carla's death, let alone a crime scene. "Maybe we should stay somewhere else."

"No need. The police finished their work at the suite and cleared the scene. It's actually very secure there. In a way, it's better. I feel secure knowing that you're all safe there."

"We're uh, in danger?"

"No—not at all. But to be honest, your association with me poses some risk. I warned Pearl about this, but she insisted it wasn't a problem."

Aunt Pearl had another problem, though. Me. I resented her lack of disclosure, and I intended to confront her about it.

"But if the police think it's an accidental drowning and it's not, that means there's a killer on the loose. Maybe Bones was taken out by the same person."

"Possible, but we'll never know."

The police could rationalize a body in a pool, but one in a borrowed coffin with a bullet in the forehead was another story. "But the police can't just dismiss—"

"The police are bought and paid for." He waved his hand in dismissal. "I know what you're thinking. Bones Battilana was an obvious hit. The police will find a way to close that case too. Maybe they'll blame it on another dead guy. Somebody wants a cut of our very lucrative business, and money talks."

"That seems a bit extreme." The Racatelli family business was never talked about in Westwick Corners, mostly because we had the vague sense that it involved illegal activities and we didn't want to get involved. Our small town operated on a "don't ask, don't tell" policy for stuff like this. Still, Rocco's direct reference to his family's dealings in the crime world surprised me.

Rocco gazed outside to the taped-off grave area. "The easiest thing for the police to do would be to compromise the crime scene. They're probably doing that right now, to eliminate any possibility of the D.A. having enough evidence to charge anyone."

"A cover-up?" I wasn't convinced that the police would purposely bungle the investigation. But maybe things operated differently in Las Vegas. "Bones had a bullet through his head. They have to at least investigate that."

Rocco nodded. "They will, but they'll do a shoddy job. Or they'll try to pin it on me."

"But what motive do you have to..." I had the answer before I finished my sentence. As Carla's new husband, Bones stood directly in Rocco's path to take over the Racatelli business. "Never mind."

"Why did Carla even have a pool if she was so deathly afraid of water?" I winced at my bad choice of words as soon as they left my mouth, but Rocco seemed oblivious.

"The penthouse suite already had the pool when we bought the hotel. She insisted on living at the hotel. You can't exactly take a pool out of a concrete high-rise. Filling it in would look ugly, so Grandma just kept it drained. Except, of course, on the very day she died. On that day the pool was full. That's why I think it was a set-up." Rocco paused and stared off into space. "At least it was me who found her."

"I'm really sorry, Rocco."

"The police can claim it was an accident, but I know better. It has to be a mob hit."

I had so many questions I didn't even know where to start. For the moment I forgot that I wanted to leave. "Maybe it's not too late to request an autopsy. Given the circumstances…" I glanced outside. Surely the discovery of Battilano warranted some further investigation, and the grave had yet to be covered over.

He shrugged, his palms extended outward. "Even if they did it, they probably wouldn't release the results. They keep stalling. I think I know why."

"We have to get an autopsy report, Rocco." Despite my plan to mind my own business, I wanted justice too.

CHAPTER 21

Despite my best intentions, I stayed at the funeral reception. I stood in a corner of the room with Rocco. I couldn't help myself. I felt myself drawn to him again. Maybe Aunt Pearl had renewed the spell. But it wasn't just my physical attraction that drew me to Rocco. Now I truly felt sorry for him.

Once the guests had paid their respects, things began to get a lot more interesting. Everyone was basically getting drunk at the bar.

Aunt Pearl and Mom didn't seem to mind. They both wavered unsteadily on their feet from too much wine.

"See that guy over there?" Rocco pointed to Aunt Pearl's boy-toy. He had left the bar and stood at the buffet table, loading his plate with a second helping of dessert. "That's Manny 'The Man' La Manna. He's trying to get rid of the competition and move in on our business."

La Manna wasn't much of a mover, even in the buffet line. He was barely over five feet tall and not enough of a physical presence to intimidate anyone, let alone move in on anyone's racket. But I supposed he probably got others to do his dirty work for him.

"That's him?" I nodded, not wanting to let on that I already knew who Manny was. I watched as he licked his fingers, then wiped his hands on his pinstriped suit. I failed to see what Aunt Pearl found so attractive about him. Aside from his dubious occupation, he had poor etiquette, something Aunt Pearl was, strangely, a stickler about. Her involvement with a crime capo freaked me out. "You think he was involved?"

"No doubt."

"What's with the all weird nicknames?"

We both watched as Manny headed back over to the bar with a heaping plateful of tiramisu.

"Everyone has a nickname. It's for protection, in case of eaves-droppers or police surveillance."

That pretty much confirmed their criminal activities, which, since this was Vegas, probably involved something like match-fixing, illegal gambling, or money laundering. It seemed insensitive to press Rocco for details at the moment, so I asked about Manny La Manna's business instead. They had to be in the same line of work, given Manny's hostile takeover plans. "What's his racket?"

"Loan sharking, extortion, money laundering, you name it. Pretty much everything that goes on here behind the scenes."

I refocused on Manny, who had stood by the bar. He attacked his tiramisu with such relish that I almost expected him to lick the plate.

The man standing next to Manny suddenly caught my attention.

"I know that man." I pointed at Christophe, who stood at Manny's elbow. "I'm surprised to see our butler at the funeral. But I suppose that makes sense. After all, he was Carla's butler."

"Butler?" Rocco frowned. "Grandma never had a butler."

"He's included with the suite. At least that's what he told us."

Rocco gave me a blank stare. "Crisco has no business being in the suite. He sure as hell ain't no butler."

"Crisco? What kind of name is that?"

"You don't want to know. Crisco works for Manny. He does all the stuff no one else will touch." Rocco scratched his chin thoughtfully. "Maybe this isn't so bad. If he's in the suite, then you can keep tabs on him."

Manny seemed to have his tentacles everywhere, and that apparently even extended to my own family. I shivered, though the crowded room was warm.

My pulse quickened. Whatever reason Christophe had for being in our suite had nothing to do with canapés or cocktails. He wanted something from us. "No. We have to get out of there. I've got to warn Mom and Aunt Pearl."

Rocco's hand clamped over my arm. "You can't do that. You'll tip him off. Besides, he's not after you. He's after me. He thinks I'll come back to the suite."

"But what if he—"

"He could care less about you and your family, Cen. No offense, but he's probably setting a trap for me. Just give me some time before you do anything. You've got to stay there. Otherwise, he'll get suspicious. Keep an eye on him until I figure out a plan. I can't let him get to me."

"That makes no sense. He's right here at the funeral. He can get to you right now if he wanted to."

Rocco steered me out into the hallway. "No one's gonna take me out in plain sight at a funeral. Too many witnesses. Besides, it's a funeral. There are some lines even wise guys won't cross."

I didn't buy Rocco's reasoning. Any self-respecting Mafioso would keep his mouth shut. If a mob hit wasn't reason enough for *omerta*, a code of silence, I didn't know what was.

Anger welled inside me. "How could you let us stay in the suite without telling us?"

"Pearl knew the plan already, and Crisco's not that big of a deal. You guys will keep tabs on him while I focus on Manny."

"I'm not so sure about that. Christophe may already have a head start on us." I flashed back to Christophe's potent wine, an excellent method to neutralize a witch or three. How had he even gained access to the suite in the first place? How long ago? Maybe Christophe had killed Carla.

Christophe might have us in his gunsights, but we could corner him too.

"Just be careful," Rocco said. "But I really need all the help I can get. Manny's plan is pretty clear. First Grandma, then Bones Battilana. That means that I'm next on his hit list. Once he gets rid of us, all Las Vegas is his for the taking."

It was a little convoluted, but Rocco seemed to know what he was talking about.

I refocused on Christophe, but he was no longer smiling at me. His smile had morphed into a frown directed at Rocco. Christophe tilted his head and spoke to Manny, who also returned the stare. Manny nudged a burly man who had joined them. The man made a cutting motion across his throat.

The three men laughed.

I got the feeling I wouldn't be enjoying any of Christophe's killer cocktails for a very long time.

CHAPTER 22

I exited the elevator behind Mom and Aunt Pearl. As I
stepped into the marble foyer, I paused. I needed a
moment to collect my thoughts. Instead, I was confronted by the
Capone-era couple in the oil painting. They seemed to stare straight
at me. Now I realized that they were probably either Carla's or
Tommy's parents. The woman's intense blue eyes were just like
Rocco's and the man looked like Rocco's twin, dressed in 1930s era
clothing.

Our suite seemed more like a prison than a refuge, but it was too
late to turn back. Like it or not, we were committed to helping
Rocco.

My shoulders relaxed as I scanned the suite. Christophe was
nowhere to be seen, but I expected him to arrive at any moment.

Chills ran down my spine. Whatever reasons Christophe had to
stick around had to be sussed out. My nerves rattled at the thought
of confronting him. It wasn't what Rocco wanted, but I needed to
know what was going on, and asking seemed to be the only option.
We needed a plan, and we needed to act quickly.

Aunt Pearl collapsed on the sofa, tired but seemingly relaxed and unworried. Mom stumbled towards the patio doors, giggly after a few too many drinks at the funeral reception.

The suite's air conditioning cooled me but did nothing to ease my frayed nerves. I headed straight upstairs, where I ditched my uncomfortable wool suit for shorts and a t-shirt. I hoisted my suitcase up onto the bed and shoved my belongings inside. I wanted to be packed and ready to leave at a moment's notice. Of course, Christophe might never return, but the odds of that were slim. Manny wanted to get rid of Rocco, and any of Rocco's confidantes were likely fair game too. We could be used as pawns, or worse. I had tried to convince Mom and Aunt Pearl of this on the way back to the hotel, but they dismissed my thoughts as ridiculous.

With or without Mom and Aunt Pearl, I was hell-bent on heading home. As far as I was concerned, Rocco was on his own. Only he could extricate himself from his chosen life of crime. I had serious reservations about leaving Mom and Aunt Pearl in the middle of a mob turf war, but I was powerless to stop them.

I flashed back to Rocco's mention of his grandmother and her cause of death. Supposedly Carla had drowned, yet she had been discovered face up in the pool. That same detail had bothered me earlier, but only now did I realize why.

Drowning victims were normally face down. Drowning necessarily involved being immersed in water, or face down. A body naturally floated in the same position as at death, unless disturbed. Dead people didn't move around unless there was a current or something else to move them.

Or somebody else.

It validated Rocco's claim. It also alarmed me, since the one person with unauthorized access to Carla's suite was due to return at any moment.

I squeezed my suitcase shut and bounded down the stairs. "Aunt Pearl!"

"Now what?"

"If you refuse to leave here, we at least need to get rid of Christophe. He can't stay with us." I recounted Rocco's claims. Now that the whole butler charade was blown, I expected something a lot more sinister from him than fancy cocktails.

Aunt Pearl laughed. "Don't be ridiculous. Chris is harmless. He just does whatever Manny tells him to."

I raised my hands in objection. "That's the whole problem. Christophe works for Manny, and Manny wants to kill Rocco." I couldn't bring myself to call him Crisco. It was just too creepy.

"—and Manny does whatever I want him to." Aunt Pearl tucked a strand of gray hair behind her ear and winked at me.

"Why are you romantically involved with a mobster?" I threw my hands in the air. "This is serious stuff, Aunt Pearl. We're in the middle of a turf war, and we're going to get hurt. You could get us all killed."

"Of course it's serious. We're here for a reason, Cen. To find and lock up the real killer."

I tilted my head towards the patio, where Mom sat at the pool, dipping her toes in the water. In the very same pool where Carla had met her end. I shivered.

"She's fine." Aunt Pearl held up a finger. "Just a sec."

I followed her into the kitchen. "Just because the police aren't doing their job doesn't mean that we have to. We could get ourselves killed. That doesn't bring Carla back."

"We'll just get things started. Give the cops a little push." She pulled two glasses out of the cupboard and snapped her fingers. A chilled pitcher of strawberry margaritas slowly solidified in front of us.

All this alcohol consumption couldn't possibly be good. It dulled our senses, as well as our supernatural powers.

Aunt Pearl poured two glasses and pushed one towards me. "The police are all the same."

I ignored both the glass and her pointed reference to Tyler. I was the only one with any sense, and I couldn't afford to have it compromised with more alcohol. "We're no match for organized crime."

"If anything, I'd call Rocco's operation 'unorganized' crime. Whoever did this has to pay, no doubt about that. Even Jimmy Hoffa never had to share a coffin." Aunt Pearl's eyes moistened as she raised her glass to her lips. She downed it in one shot and slammed the glass down on the counter. "Where do I even start?"

I beckoned for her to follow and we headed back into the living room. I glanced outside where Mom still sat by the pool. Mom looked contented and relaxed, not heartbroken. Though in hindsight she had been acting a little strange for the last few days. "Tell me quick, before Mom comes back inside."

Mom and Aunt Pearl's stories didn't jive, so one or possibly both were not telling me the truth.

Aunt Pearl rolled her eyes. "Like I told you before, Bones sure found a way into Carla's heart. He swept her off her feet and married her, all in the space of about three weeks."

I shook my head. "Mom's bound to find out about all this. It will be in the news."

"Yes. Carla's secret marriage will be exposed. So will the fact that all of Carla Racatelli's holdings became community property."

"Bones inherited instead of Rocco?" I gasped. "You mean she kept the casino in her own name, rather than a corporation? How could she be so—?"

"Stupid? I don't know, Cen. Love makes everybody act stupid sometimes. That Danny was a real charmer. You couldn't really appreciate the effect he has on women until you met him in person. Of course, it's too late for that now." She reached into her purse and pulled out a photograph. "These guys don't like getting their picture taken, but I managed to get one of all of us, out on a double date. This was just months before Danny left Ruby for Carla."

I snatched the picture from her. Mom and Aunt Pearl were at a

Vegas floor show. They sat at a front row table with two men. One was Manny La Manna, and the other, Danny "Bones" Battilana, sans forehead bullet hole.

Manny sat beside Aunt Pearl, casually dressed in a sports shirt, while Bones was impeccably tailored in a white linen shirt and blazer. He smiled warmly at the camera, his arm draped around Mom. She leaned into him, beaming with love and happiness.

My pulse quickened. Despite Mom's denial, it appeared that she and Bones had, at the very least, a romantic relationship. And they both appeared to be happy. Yet within months, Bones had apparently married Carla. I needed that margarita after all. I raised my glass and took a sip.

"What did Rocco think when Bones started dating his grandma?"

"He wasn't happy about it. He tried to warn Carla. She wouldn't listen, thinking Rocco was just upset about her dating again."

"Rocco had a reason to kill Bones," I said. "He wanted control."

Aunt Pearl nodded. "Rocco resisted, and that's what started the lobby gunfight. Bones wanted to scare off the Hotel Babylon's employees and replace them with his own people. Then he would control everything."

"Seems like that didn't work out very well for Bones. Only Bones wasn't in the lobby this morning. He was already dead." I frowned. "If he was already dead, why the gunfight?"

Aunt Pearl shrugged. "His guys were just carrying out his instructions."

I flashed back to the corpse. "They must have been old instructions, because Bones looked like he had been dead for a while." My hand flew to my mouth. "Rocco could have killed Bones. He has a motive."

"True."

"You don't seem all that concerned."

"I'm more concerned about who died first, Bones or Carla," Aunt Pearl said. "If Bones was killed in revenge for Carla, then Rocco has a problem. That would mean that Bones had outlived Carla. He would become Carla's heir, not Rocco. But I'm sure you'll prove otherwise."

"Me?"

"You're good at this investigating stuff, and you have an in with the police. You'll have us out of trouble in no time."

It was the one and only time Aunt Pearl had brought up Sheriff Tyler Gates, and I wasn't sure why. He worked in Westwick Corners, not Las Vegas, so I couldn't see what that had to do with anything.

"No, Aunt Pearl. We really need to get out of here." I lowered my voice to a whisper. "What about Christophe? That guy scares me."

"Don't be silly. Christophe is far too busy whipping up cocktails and appetizers to plan murders. He could really give Ruby a run for her money on the hospitality side, though."

I imagined Christophe bartending for us in Westwick Corners, then just as quickly shoved it out of my mind. "That's ridiculous. I don't like you fraternizing with these mobsters. It's dangerous."

"You're overreacting. Crisc—I mean, Christophe—is just here to protect us, Cen. Manny sent him to stand guard over us."

"You're sure about that? This suite has a lot of security and I'll bet Rocco—"

"Rocco doesn't know what he's doing right now. He's too distracted. Besides, I didn't say I believed Manny. I'm just going along with him so I don't blow my cover."

"What—now you're some sort of secret agent?"

"You catch on quick, Cen." Aunt Pearl rolled her eyes. "We keep our friends close, and our enemies closer."

CHAPTER 23

Aunt Pearl stared off into space. "Ruby never wanted you to find out about Danny, but it's not like I have anyone else to confide in." She drew up her legs and slid close enough that I could smell the alcohol on her breath. "We have to tell Ruby the truth about her boyfriend. It's gonna hurt, but maybe she will see the bright side. Bones was seeing Carla on the sly, but only to take advantage of her casino as a means to launder money."

"I don't see how his ulterior motive to launder money will make her feel any better." I flashed back to the funeral reception. Finding out your boyfriend had married someone else would ruin anyone's day. "Mom will still be upset. Why do we have to tell her anything? He's dead now, so none of that really matters anymore."

"Of course it matters," Aunt Pearl snapped. "Now let's get back to Carla. She stopped Danny from laundering his money."

"I can see why," I said. "Carla probably had her own money to launder. Adding more might get her caught." Great. Now I was thinking like a criminal. "Bones was smart to marry Carla. As his wife, she would never have to testify against him in court."

"Look where that got him, Cen. The guy's dead." Aunt Pearl sniffled. "Bones isn't really Carla's husband. Never was."

"But the Las Vegas wedding—"

"All a sham. Carla is—I mean, was—a smart cookie." Aunt Pearl's eyes moistened and her voice broke. "She knew exactly what Bones was up to. That's why she got the idea of a fake wedding. Bones would think they were married, and that bought Carla some time. She wanted to avoid an all-out turf war."

"That worked out really well."

"She let Danny wine and dine her, all the while knowing he wanted in on the action. Then she arranged a quickie wedding, complete with witnesses and fake paperwork. Only he thought it was real. It seemed like a good idea," Aunt Pearl said. "But maybe it was too little, too late."

"Bones—I mean Danny—must have somehow found out and knocked her off."

Aunt Pearl sniffled. "Who knows? We still don't have any solid proof pointing to anyone. Bones had reason to, but his death provides a rock solid alibi."

"Depends on the timing." It was true that Bones' corpse had been in much rougher shape than Carla's, but maybe there was a good reason. "Carla's body was embalmed, but I'm guessing that Bones didn't get the same treatment: his body was just dumped in the bottom of Carla's casket."

"So?"

"He looks like he died earlier, but that's only because he didn't get the post-mortem embalming, make-up, and whatever else the morticians do." I glanced outside, alarmed that Mom had vanished from view. I took a deep breath, thinking I was overreacting. The patio wrapped around the suite on three sides, so she was probably just out of sight, enjoying the view.

I turned back to Aunt Pearl. "I wish they would do an autopsy on Carla. Drowning just doesn't make sense."

"That's easy to arrange. Your wish is my command." Aunt Pearl waved a hand in the air and looked towards the ceiling. "I see you're finally on board, Cen. Better late than never."

A sheaf of papers fell from above and landed in my lap. I shuffled the papers into order. "Did you just make this up?

"Don't be ridiculous. I would never do that."

"But the medical examiner didn't—"

"Did so. The autopsy was covered up, just like everything else."

I held up the autopsy report. "Where did you get this?"

Aunt Pearl just rolled her eyes. "Doesn't matter. You read that while I do a little sleuthing in the casino."

"No gambling, Aunt Pearl. You know what it does to you." Aunt Pearl's impulsiveness and her gambling problem were a deadly combination. Even if her winning lottery ticket was real, she had probably spent a small fortune to get it. Witches could conjure up just about anything except cold, hard cash. A winning lottery ticket was pretty much the same as cash though. Conjuring one up was akin to supernatural forgery. That was a serious enough breach to warrant a lifetime WICCA ban.

My aunt broke small rules here and there, but she would never jeopardize her witch status, no matter what. On the other hand, compulsive gamblers had to feed their addiction, so maybe it was beyond her control.

Aunt Pearl shrugged. "Whatever. I can take it or leave it. But don't forget: I'm a lottery winner. I can afford to gamble if I want to."

I was about to ask Aunt Pearl for the umpteenth time how much she had won when Mom screamed.

"Help!"

We both rushed outside to find Mom waist-deep in the pool. Her hair was soaked, and her mascara was smeared down her cheeks. She must have somehow fallen into the water.

"How did you—?" I reached out my hand.

"I don't know. I somehow dozed off, I guess. Next thing I knew, I was face down in the pool." Mom's speech slurred and her teeth chattered despite the heat.

We pulled her from the pool and Aunt Pearl grabbed a towel to wrap around Mom's shoulders.

Mom lurched to one side. "Ouch...I think I twisted my ankle when I fell in."

The poolside mishap was further proof that Mom wasn't her normal, careful self, though I couldn't recall her drinking more than a glass or two at the funeral. Certainly not enough to pass out, though she had been unsteady on her feet. Whatever the reason, it was totally out of character.

I shuddered at the close call. One pool accident was enough. If that's really what had happened.

Aunt Pearl and I each took an arm and walked Mom to the sofa, where she promptly passed out. At least she was breathing normally. I placed a pillow behind her head and covered her with a blanket.

I refocused on Carla's autopsy results. It was dry reading, especially since I was unfamiliar with many of the medical terms. One thing was clear, though. Carla's true cause of death was not drowning.

According to the report, Carla's lungs contained no water, which meant that she had already been dead by the time she entered the pool. I skimmed the report until I reached the section that indicated the cause of death. The medical examiner had ruled her death a homicide, by strangulation.

I glanced up at Aunt Pearl, who was putting on her shoes, ready to go to the casino. "Wait. Have you read this?"

"How could I have read it? You've had it the whole time." She walked back over to the sofa and perched on the armrest beside me. "Why?"

"Look at this." I pointed to the section indicating the cause of death. "Carla was strangled. The pool accident was staged, to make it look like she drowned."

"I already told you that it was a cover-up. It was no accident."

"I know you did, Aunt Pearl, but I had just assumed the autopsy results had ruled her death an accident too." I held up the papers. "This proves a cover-up, but only by the police, not the medical examiner. How and why are the police covering this up?" I turned to Aunt Pearl, keeping my voice low so I didn't wake up Mom.

"They've been paid off."

"That may be so, but why isn't the medical examiner speaking up?"

Aunt Pearl shrugged. "She was paid off too."

I shook my head. "No. If she was, the autopsy report would have ruled her death an accident. We better go pay the medical examiner a visit."

Aunt Pearl's eyes widened. "She's in danger too."

I nodded as I checked my watch. It was already after 7p.m. "It's after hours, so I suppose it will have to wait until tomorrow."

"In the meantime, we better protect Rocco," Aunt Pearl said. "I put a protective shield around him for the next twenty-four hours. Only another witch can break it."

Aunt Pearl was obstinate and unstoppable when she had a goal, and tonight was no different.

"Rocco doesn't need protecting, Aunt Pearl. Stop and think about it. People are dropping like flies, yet he escapes unscathed. Why?" Now that my aunt's attraction spell had worn off, I could think more clearly. Either Aunt Pearl had a Teflon shield around him, or he was somehow involved.

"Just lucky so far, I guess." Aunt Pearl avoided my gaze. "But luck only carries a person so far."

"It's not luck. He's probably involved somehow, at least in Bones' death."

"How can you accuse poor Rocco? He's just another victim in all this." She shook her head, disappointed.

"You're not being objective, Aunt Pearl. Your emotions are getting the better of you."

Aunt Pearl stood before me. "I have to honor my promise, Cen. It was Carla's dying wish that I take care of Rocco."

I shook my head as I flashed back to Rocco and his armed bodyguards. "Rocco doesn't need you. He's old enough to take care of himself. Wait a minute. Aren't you his—"

"Godmother." Aunt Pearl finished my sentence. "Once we solve this thing and lock up the killer, we need to get Rocco back on his feet. He's gonna need my advice in his new role as head of the Racatelli family business."

I seriously hoped she meant a fairy godmother and not a godmother in the mafia sense. Aunt Pearl as a crime don, or donna, if that was how you said it in Italian, was a downright scary proposition.

"The Racatelli crime syndicate isn't a regular business, Aunt Pearl. I doubt Carla wanted you to mentor him in that." It saddened me that it had taken Carla's death to talk openly about the Racatelli family's criminal ventures. "These are dangerous people you're messing with."

"Not as dangerous as a witch with a vendetta. That's where you come in." Aunt Pearl rubbed her palms together. "You'll keep Rocco busy while I work my magic."

I held my hands up in protest. "Oh no. I am not getting involved in any of this. You're taking the whole godmother bit way too seriously."

Aunt Pearl stood defiantly in front of me, hands on hips. "I am not a godmother in the normal sense, Cendrine. Carla appointed me after Rocco's parents died when he was already in his teens. She knew she wouldn't live forever. Rocco, as her business successor, had to be ready. She figured I was the woman for the job."

"You're not exactly young yourself," I pointed out. Aunt Pearl was also in her seventies, only a couple of years younger than Carla. Her succession planning story sounded like a gross exaggeration or an outright lie.

Still, I couldn't think of anyone more focused than my aunt, so that part at least made sense. But what did she know about the inner workings of organized crime? Nothing, as far as I knew. "I think you're reading more into this than there is. If you're his godmother, aren't you technically the interim head of the Racatelli enterprise?"

Aunt Pearl nodded. "That's why we all had to come to Vegas. All of us are needed to ensure Rocco's success."

"Why me? I don't have very strong powers." And the last thing I wanted was to help a criminal tighten his grip on power. Childhood friend or not, it didn't matter.

"Exactly."

I waited for Aunt Pearl to elaborate, or at least lecture me on applying myself, but she didn't. "Not magic, but you have very strong powers of attraction."

"Powers of attract—oh no. You are not setting me up with Rocco." Using me as some sort of decoy was insulting, to say the least. Then my thoughts drifted to the lobby encounter. That muscled chest and piercing blue eyes…

Damn. What the heck was wrong with me? I wanted Tyler, not Rocco. I was certain of that. And yet my magnetic attraction to Rocco seemed to play havoc with my emotions.

"You're precisely the sort of distraction Rocco needs right now. You'll also be nearby for his safety. You can protect him in case anything goes wrong."

"Like what?" I grew uneasy.

"I don't know, Cen." Aunt Pearl paused and chose her words carefully. "Remember, only a witch can break through the protective shield I placed on Rocco. You're not the best witch—not by a mile—but at least you can jump into action if needed."

"Wait—what kind of action?"

"No time to get into details. You'll know it if it's necessary."

"Maybe I'll refuse."

"You can't. What's done is done, Cen. There's not a lot you can do about it. Just trust me on this."

"You put another attraction spell on me!" Once again I felt that strange attraction to my childhood friend. If only I had practiced my magic; then I might have been able to counter my aunt's spell. She had used me for her own ends and managed to teach me a lesson at the same time. All because I had neglected my witchcraft practice, which rendered me defenseless against my powerful aunt.

I had to become a better witch, if only to counteract Aunt Pearl's manipulation. She had tricked me again. I glared at her. "Remove the spell right now."

"No, missy. Not until we catch Carla's killer and make sure the Racatelli empire stays in Rocco's hands."

"I'm sure Rocco would rather you not interfere." I didn't want her to either. Things could go bad very quickly.

"Doesn't matter. There are uh—business issues that Rocco's not aware of yet. Personal issues too." Aunt Pearl's expression was blank. "Carla had some trouble in the relationship department."

"Those problems disappeared when she died."

"You would think so, but…"

"But what?"

"Carla was romantically involved with someone else. In a moment of passion, she may have done something she regretted."

"Another man besides Bones? Where did she find time for all this?" Carla simultaneously ran a multi-million-dollar criminal enterprise, fended off mobsters, and juggled multiple men. I managed about a tenth of what she did, and I was about fifty years younger. I was a failure compared to her. On the other hand, I was alive.

"She managed somehow."

"Who was it—another crime boss?" I was half-joking.

"Uh-huh. Manny," Aunt Pearl said.

"Your Manny?"

Aunt Pearl nodded. "She and Manny tied the knot, and this time the marriage was real."

"But you and Manny…"

"All an act. I knew Manny had secretly married Carla, but he didn't know that I knew. He still doesn't."

"Aren't you jealous?"

Aunt Pearl shrugged. "Not really. I just wanted a fling. No messy commitments."

I covered my ears, not wanting to hear more details. Images popped up in my head uninvited. "Why was Carla so eager to get married again? She was single for decades."

"You think you kids are the only ones who enjoy a little romance? Carla was mature all right, but she wasn't too old for a little fun now and again." Aunt Pearl sighed. "That's the whole problem. She got swept up in a wave of passion and forgot to get a prenup. So her death means that everything goes to Manny La Manna. Including this hotel."

Carla's Mafioso boy toy was suddenly a lot richer. "Then Manny must have killed her."

"Maybe. I honestly don't know what to think," she said. "I wouldn't put it past him, though. She was probably worth about fifty million. Then there are all of the Racatelli holdings she controlled…" Aunt Pearl's eyes grew wet with tears. "Carla would be mortified by all this fighting."

"Let's call the police and let them deal with it. Tell them about your suspicions."

Aunt Pearl shook her head emphatically. "Absolutely not. We can't involve them because Carla has a lot of illegal enterprises going on. We can't tell Ruby either. She disapproves of the shady world the Racatellis operate in."

"Of course we have to tell her." I doubted Mom was oblivious to Carla's line of work. She was just too polite to say anything about it.

One thing I was sure of was that Aunt Pearl was in more danger than she realized.

Carla's death changed more than Rocco's or Manny's future. It also called into question Aunt Pearl's involvement with Manny. And Christophe's business being in our suite.

CHAPTER 24

$\mathcal{A}$unt Pearl and I sat on the sofa, while Mom dozed peacefully at the other end. Wilt sat a few feet away at a small desk. He was bent over, his head in his hands, dejected. If I could have, I would have done a rewind spell just to make him feel better. But it didn't solve a thing. Jimmy would still come looking for him to recoup his poker losses no matter what.

Christophe had returned to the suite just minutes ago, acting as if the whole funeral scene had never happened. He went straight to the kitchen, which suited me fine.

After five minutes of banging cupboards and rattling dishes, he emerged with a tray of snacks and set it down on the coffee table in front of us. "Anyone hungry?"

I wasn't very good at small talk at the best of times, and making small talk with one of Manny La Manna's cronies made me uneasy. I was so worried about saying the wrong thing, so I just grunted thanks and speared a piece of cheese.

"What time is it?" Mom rose to a sitting position and glanced around the suite. She stood, forgetting her sore ankle. She quickly collapsed back on the sofa, a grimace of pain on her face. "I wish I could make it back out to the pool. It's so relaxing."

"I really don't think that's a good idea, Mom."

"Let me handle this." Christophe swooped Mom up in his arms like a romance novel hero and carried her over to a comfy looking divan by the window. He set her down gently and handed her a fluffy white towel. "You can at least admire the view from here."

Mom giggled, clearly enjoying Christophe's attentions. "I think I'm fine. Maybe just a little bruised from the fall."

Christophe's dimples deepened as he smiled. He acted as if nothing out of the ordinary had happened. "May I offer you ladies a beverage? You must be tired from the funeral." He winked at Mom.

Mom blushed. "Why not?"

I followed Aunt Pearl to the sofa, keeping my voice low. "Why is he keeping up the butler act? He knows we saw him with Manny."

"Sssh." Aunt Pearl drew a finger to her lips.

Christophe ignored us and kept his gaze on Mom. "I'll get some ice for your ankle."

"Cosmo for me, Chris," Aunt Pearl called after Christophe as he headed for the kitchen. "Make it a white wine for Ruby."

Mom remained silent, which I took for agreement.

"I'll just have some water. It's not even five yet," I protested.

"We're on Vegas time, Cen. This city never sleeps and neither should you. Let your hair down for a change." Aunt Pearl ran a hand through her gray hair. "Act your age for once."

Christophe disappeared around a corner and reappeared in what seemed like seconds with a large tray laden with chilled drinks and several plates of cheese, savory tarts and crackers. He handed me a glass of chilled white wine. "I took the liberty of choosing a very nice Sonoma Valley Chardonnay for you, Cendrine. Since Pearl and Ruby are having alcohol and all, I thought you might want some too."

My willpower faltered. I accepted the wine from Christophe's tray and took a sip. The Chardonnay felt smooth on my tongue and whetted my appetite. I nibbled on a piece of cheese and was overcome with exhaustion. I was too tired to care about anything anymore. We had driven all night to get here, only to face a gunfight, gambling gangsters, and murder. I hadn't slept for over twenty-four hours, and I no longer had the energy to protest Aunt Pearl's plans, or even keep an eye on Christophe.

"You're sure fast on your feet, Chris." Aunt Pearl gulped her Cosmo and slammed her empty glass down on the coffee table. "You magic or something?"

I choked on my drink, spewing Chardonnay all over my clothes. I recovered and scowled at my aunt, annoyed at her supernatural references.

If Christophe was offended, he didn't show it. "It's a trade secret. I can also make dinner arrangements if you wish." He stood and awaited our instructions. Maybe he wasn't a gangster after all.

"I wish, Chris, thanks!" Aunt Pearl jumped to her feet. "I think we'll stay in for dinner, though. Why don't you surprise us?"

"Fine. I'll just run out and pick up a few things for dinner." Christophe headed out into the foyer, his rubber soles squeaking on the marble floor.

I waited until the elevator door closed and turned to my aunt.

"If he really works for Manny, we don't want him coming back."

Mom sipped her wine and pulled her plush white robe around her, oblivious to our dilemma.

"Fine, we'll bolt the door or something." Aunt Pearl shook her head slowly. "I know one way you could stop him from coming back here."

"Whatever it is, I'll do it. How?"

Aunt Pearl smiled. "A protection spell around the perimeter. Did you practice that one? Or have you been too busy with other things?"

She also knew that I hadn't practiced, and now she was about to make me pay for that transgression. Again.

"Can't you—"

"No, Cen. You must stand on your own two feet."

"We're in a serious situation here. Can't you make an exception just this once?"

She dismissed me with a wave of her hand. "What better way to learn? At least you're motivated now."

I sighed. "Your tough love is just getting us into all sorts of trouble. At least do it for Mom."

"You worry too much, Cen. Just enjoy the suite, because you'll probably never stay in a place this nice this again."

"We could stay in the RV," I said.

Aunt Pearl wagged her finger. "You'd feel safer in a tin can in the underground parking lot? Not a smart move when the mob's after you."

She had a point, and it was too late to do anything about the room tonight. "Let's just stick out the night here. We'll stay inside and then check out tomorrow."

"I'm not hanging out here. This is Vegas, baby. I'm going downstairs to the casino. Care to join me?"

I shook my head, only to discover that Aunt Pearl had already disappeared up the spiral staircase to the bedrooms.

Maybe Aunt Pearl was right to make the best of a bad situation, but all I really wanted to do was go to bed. Aunt Pearl's so-called mission just didn't seem like that big of a deal anymore.

With the funeral over, there wasn't much else that could happen before we left tomorrow. What could possibly go wrong?

I sipped my wine and glanced at Mom, who had fallen asleep once again. She snored softly on the divan. I walked over and carefully removed the empty wineglass from her hand and placed it on a side table. I adjusted the pillows elevating her swollen ankle and felt my eyes grow heavy.

Mom's lack of consciousness and my lack of magic skills left us pretty much defenseless, and Aunt Pearl was well aware of that. Still, she wouldn't let us stay here if we were really in danger. For all the trouble she caused, she was loyal and protective.

But maybe Aunt Pearl was right. If I had to be stranded, there were a lot worse places to be than surrounded by luxury and being waited on hand and foot. It was my last thought as sleep overtook me.

CHAPTER 25

I jerked awake on the sofa, disoriented. Judging by the dim light outside, it was dusk. I must have dozed off. I lifted my head towards the direction of the sound.

Thump.

Thump, thump, thump.

I couldn't remember falling asleep, though I must have, because I felt completely out of it. I also had a pounding headache, though I remembered having only a few sips of wine. The alcohol, combined with dehydration and too much sun at the funeral, had done me in.

The hotel suite key card was still clutched in my hand and I realized in a panic that I hadn't called Tyler since returning from the funeral. It was that stupid Rocco spell. Half the time I couldn't think straight, and the rest of the time was spent keeping tabs on Aunt Pearl.

Another broken promise.

Thump, thump.

Any chance I had with the man I had lusted after for months now was probably blown. All because of my interfering aunt and her kidnapping stunt.

I was now convinced that she knew of our date all along. She would do anything to drive him away, and that included sabotaging our fledgling relationship any way she could. The Racatelli affair just happened to be a convenient excuse.

Thump, thump.

Aunt Pearl's dislike for Tyler wasn't personal. She just found him frustrating because she had met her match. He was the only sheriff she couldn't run out of town. She had probably kidnapped me on purpose to thwart any chance of romance.

Thump.

As my eyes gradually adjusted to the darkness, I turned my gaze towards the direction of the noise. My gaze traveled up the spiral staircase and came to rest on a pair of stiletto heels attached to shapely legs.

"You-hoo! How do I look?" Aunt Pearl's voice echoed against the high ceiling as her manicured hand gripped the spiral staircase railing. From my vantage point on the downstairs sofa, I saw only the bottom half of a crimson red sequined evening gown, shimmering under the halogen lights.

I bolted upright and swore under my breath as I absorbed the scene. My brief carefree mood from earlier had vanished. It wasn't Aunt Pearl at all. It was Carolyn Conroe. "You can't pull off a Carolyn here."

Carolyn Conroe was Aunt Pearl's alter ego, a magical Marilyn Monroe clone that my aunt shape-shifted into whenever she wanted to have some fun. Carolyn was even more reckless than Aunt Pearl, with a devious, unpredictable side. The thought of Carolyn unchecked and unsupervised in Las Vegas terrified me.

"Why not? Carolyn loves Vegas even more than I do." A thigh-high slit exposed shapely legs as Aunt Pearl—or rather Carolyn—slowly and stiffly descended the stairs in her impossibly high heels.

Carolyn's youth was only skin-deep; it still had to be carried on

Aunt Pearl's seventy-year-old arthritic legs. Even witchcraft couldn't cover all the bases.

"What happens in Vegas, stays in Vegas." She stopped a few stairs from the bottom and winked. "*Project Vegas Vendetta*, phase two."

"What about Christophe? You can't pull your shenanigans with him around. He can't find out that we're witches." I had no idea when he planned to return. Since we had only arrived this morning, I had no idea whether he was a live-in butler, or if he clocked off at the end of his workday.

Aunt Pearl shook her head as she reached the staircase bottom. "Who cares? We'll never see him again after this weekend. If he sees Carolyn, just tell him she's a friend of yours."

Like I had any choice. "What about Wilt?"

"Wilt's so gambling-obsessed that he won't notice a thing. Stop worrying about other people, Cen. Sheesh." Carolyn grabbed a silver clutch purse off the coffee table and snapped it open as she walked towards the foyer. She puckered her lips and applied crimson lipstick. "I've got to run."

Aunt Pearl's happy mood seemed out of place for someone grieving their recently departed friend. I glanced beside me on the sofa, where Mom was still passed out, oblivious to our conversation. "I see you're still mourning."

"Carla would absolutely love my disguise," she said. "Don't worry, though, I'll be mourning as my regular self. I just need to unwind a little in the casino first."

"Change back before someone sees you." My head pounded, like a bad hangover. I glanced at my half-full margarita on the coffee table. Christophe wasn't the only one spiking drinks. I suspected Aunt Pearl had fortified my margarita with something.

"Girls just wanna have fun, Cen. Don't be such a downer. Join me."

My head throbbed as I stood. Aunt Pearl seemed completely unaffected, though she had much more to drink than I. I pointed to

Mom on the sofa. "I can't leave Mom like this. Whatever she drank at the funeral really did a number on her."

Carolyn ignored me and hobbled to the door in her four-inch heels.

"Aunt Pearl?" I jumped from my seat and joined her in the foyer. "How long will you be gone?"

"Depends on what kind of action's going on downstairs."

"What if Christophe comes back?"

She rolled her eyes. "I don't know. Get him to mix you some drinks, make dinner, whatever. Just keep him busy."

I threw my hands in the air. "You can't just leave us here. You tricked me into coming under false pretenses. I already missed my job interview and a date. I'm not putting up with any more of your crazy stuff."

"All we did was attend a funeral. I admit it's not every day that someone drops the casket, but, all in all, I thought things went okay."

"You're changing the subject." I stomped my foot. "You did this on purpose, just to ruin my chance of a normal job and to stop me from dating Tyler." I knew she knew, I might as well say it.

"Oh, Cendrine! Quit your whining. Stop obsessing over that man. He's not worth it." She placed her hands on her hips. "Why did you bother coming here in the first place?"

"You kidnapped me, remember?"

Carolyn batted her false eyelashes. "You're being overly dramatic. Everything isn't always all about you, you know."

My mouth dropped open. "Me? You're the drama queen."

"You're right. I am." She smirked. "Maybe it would be best if you went back to Westwick Corners after all. We'll talk more when I get back."

"You'll help me with a spell?" I brightened at the thought. A little magic help from Aunt Pearl and I could teleport back home in minutes. I could be back in my own bed tonight.

"Why don't you practice your magic and we'll see what we can do when I get back."

"Can't we do it now?"

Carolyn tapped her watch. "Sorry, no time. Maybe later. I've got stuff I need to deal with before it's too late."

My shoulders slumped in disappointment as I watched her leave. I padded back into the living room, thinking that worst-case scenario, I could catch a flight home. Maybe not tonight, but tomorrow morning. I'd borrow Mom's credit card and pay her back later. I could be home in hours.

I brightened as I spied Mom's laptop on the dining room table and flipped it open. My hopes quickly vanished when I discovered that the suite had no Internet. It was probably related to the "no phones" rule. There had to be wireless in the lobby. Maybe even a tour operator who could book me a flight home.

Mom snored peacefully on the sofa, her swollen ankle propped up on pillows. It seemed a shame to wake her up, but I also hesitated to leave her alone.

I brightened at the realization that she had a butler at her disposal. Christophe would return soon and could get her anything she needed for the short time I was away. Whether he worked for Manny or not, he seemed to treat us, and especially Mom, well.

Except for his killer cocktails, I reminded myself.

It wasn't ideal to leave Mom, but the idea of leaving Aunt Pearl to her own devices was even worse.

I scribbled a note and left it on the coffee table in case Mom woke up, then headed down to the casino.

CHAPTER 26

I didn't get far before I ran into Rocco at the bar. He occupied the same table as before. He sat with his back to the wall, which gave him a clear view of all the comings and goings in the lobby. That included me. He caught my eye and beckoned me over.

My pulse quickened as my eyes locked on his. Spell or not, my attraction to him was overpowering. Judging by his gaze, it seemed to be mutual. Despite my awareness of Aunt Pearl's trickery, I was powerless to fight it.

"Cen—we need to talk." He motioned for me to sit.

I took my seat, eyeing the same two thugs seated at the next table. It felt like déjà vu, though it made sense when you thought about it. As the hotel owner, Rocco had his own permanently reserved table.

Rocco downed his drink and leaned closer. "Grandma's death was no accident. She had plenty of enemies, people with enough power to stop an investigation. Trouble is, the police are bought and paid for."

The irony of a criminal complaining about police corruption struck me. "By whom?"

"Uncle Manny. I think he's behind Grandma's death." Rocco's eyes grew wistful. "He's not actually my blood relative, but before the turf war started, our families were quite close. That all changed as Uncle Manny's ambitions grew. It created a rift between our families. It's one thing to fight over territory, but I never expected him to kill for it."

That was exactly what crime families did, as far as I knew. Rocco was obviously in denial. I didn't know exactly what sort of rackets the Racatellis were involved in, and I didn't want to know, either. But like it or not, Aunt Pearl had already involved me. "Carla obviously knew the risks involved in criminal activities."

Rocco nodded. "She did, but she just wanted to make a little more money for a comfortable retirement. For her and me both, since I wanted out of the family business too. I planned to keep the hotel and other investments, but get rid of the shadier side businesses and go straight. Grandma tried to strike a deal with Manny, so we could go legit. But he wanted more. In this business, there's only one way out. In a casket."

Rocco made no mention of Manny and Carla's secret wedding, so I wasn't sure if he knew about it. If not, I didn't want to be the one to break it to him.

"You think Manny was responsible for Carla's death?" The circumstances surrounding her death were certainly suspicious, but they didn't necessarily point to Manny. "Does he have an alibi?"

"He says he was at the casino, but I've gone through all the surveillance footage and there's no sign of him. Yet he has a bunch of witnesses who said he was in a high-stakes poker game. Based on my video, they are obviously lying."

"You told the police about this?"

"Of course, but they just discounted it. They still think it was an accident so they aren't even investigating."

I suddenly remembered the autopsy report I had left lying on the coffee table upstairs. What if Christophe returned to the suite and discovered it?

I stood. "Something's come up. I've got to go, Rocco."

"No—wait." He grabbed my wrist, but just as quickly released it. "I think I can get them to open up the case."

"That's great." I stepped back.

"Yes and no. If they do investigate and have to pin a murder on somebody, they'll arrest me instead of Manny. I have no alibi, and everything to gain from Grandma's death. I'd inherit everything."

I shook my head. Poor Rocco really was in the dark. "That's not reason enough. They need evidence against you."

"Apparently they already have something, or at least a motive."

"You? But why—"

"They'll claim I was tired of waiting for Grandma to retire. Not only that, but I'd benefit from her demise. True, I'd inherit everything, but she shared everything with me already. I don't know the business like she did, and the last thing I wanted—even from a business perspective—is for her to be gone. I can't possibly run things as well as she did, not even close. But maybe with your help…" Rocco's voice broke.

"I'm sorry, Rocco. I really don't see how I can help. You need a lawyer, not a small town reporter." An unemployable reporter at that. I stood.

"No—Cen, wait. See, I know your family secrets, just like you know mine. You're the only one that can help me, Cen. If I can't crack the corruption, I need help to expose it. Exactly the kind of help you can give me, as a witch."

My mouth dropped open as I realized Rocco knew exactly the extent of the West family's secret. "A spell isn't going to bring Carla back, Rocco."

"I know that, but maybe you can help me another way. Finding proof that Manny wasn't where he said he was."

"I don't see how…"

"You can go back in time, retrace his steps, and see exactly the events leading up to the murder. Then we can tear apart his alibi in another way, make the police act on it."

"What makes you think I can do that?"

"Pearl did a rewind spell for me once. As a favor when I lost a bunch of money that wasn't mine. She saved my life that day."

Aunt Pearl breaking the rules as usual. "Then why don't you ask Aunt Pearl to help?"

"I can't," Rocco said. "She's still very upset about Grandma. I don't want to expose her to the truth about how Grandma actually died. Whatever that turns out to be."

I turned around to look for any sign of Carolyn Conroe, but my aunt's alter-ego was nowhere to be found. Which was good in a way, since she wasn't exactly the grieving friend Rocco thought she was.

"I'd like to help, but truth is that I'm not a very good witch. Especially not with rewind spells. That's pretty advanced magic." Technically I could do a spell, but plenty could go wrong. It seemed like a bad idea to mix magic with mobsters. In truth, it scared me half to death. If I did it well, then Rocco would want repeat favors. And if I failed, who knew what the repercussions might be?

"I have faith in you, Cen. In fact, you're the only person I can trust right now."

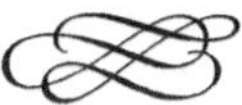

CHAPTER 27

I left the bar after convincing Rocco to first call a lawyer and then pay the medical examiner a visit.

Maybe he could coax the truth out of the medical examiner. I hoped he could uncover the truth himself, without resorting to extreme measures. If only he could get a copy of that autopsy report the legitimate way. Then it would help both of us. It was worth a try.

If he couldn't get answers, he could request to have Carla's body exhumed for a second autopsy, but that was something I didn't want to even think about right now.

The death by drowning diagnosis was very troubling. I flashed back to the coffin fiasco. Aside from the lack of water in Carla's lungs, her serene expression was a dead giveaway. Drowning victims were never expressionless. Their facial expressions were inevitably ones of terror and desperation, frozen at the final moment when they realized that they had just lost the final fight of their life.

Suddenly I felt very sad. Whatever Carla's deeds in life, they weren't bad enough to end this way. I also felt sorry for my aunt at losing her lifelong friend, even if she chose inappropriate ways to express her sorrow.

Then there were my strange feelings for Rocco. I had never been attracted to him, yet I found myself thinking about him constantly. Almost as much as I thought about Tyler, in fact.

Tyler.

He had warned me not to get involved, and he was right. I should just go upstairs, enjoy our luxury suite, and watch over Mom until she woke up. Aunt Pearl's promise to get me back home almost certainly came with strings attached, but at the moment it was my only viable option.

I walked in a daze, still trying to decide whether to track down Aunt Pearl and bail her out of whatever trouble she had found, or just go back upstairs to our suite. I was torn. Soon I found myself a few feet from the lobby elevators where a crowd had gathered.

I craned my neck to get a better look at the source of the excitement. The whistles and excited murmurs from the crowd made me guess that a rock star or Hollywood A-lister was in our midst. I wondered who was performing in the show lounge tonight.

A flash of red sequins and long blonde hair caught my eye and I got a sick feeling.

My fears were realized as Aunt Pearl—or rather her alter-ego, Carolyn Conroe—came into view. She twirled a rhinestone necklace around her fingers as she sang *Diamonds Are a Girl's Best Friend* in a sultry voice.

"Who is she?" A teenage girl handed me her phone and pointed to her and her mom. "Will you take our picture?"

Great. Aunt Pearl had not only morphed into her Carolyn Conroe shtick, but she flaunted it, pretending to be a celebrity to boot. I took a couple of pictures of the girl and her mom on either side of a smirking Carolyn before handing the girl's phone back.

I glared at Carolyn, annoyed at her fan club just as much as my misplaced pity. She seemed oblivious to the events swirling around us. Instead, she just seemed like she was out to have a good time.

Carolyn winked saucily.

I closed my hand around Carolyn's arm and steered her away from the crowd. "We need to talk."

"Don't you ever have any fun?" Carolyn swore under her breath. "Whatever happens in Vegas, stays in Vegas. You know that."

I ignored her comment and gripped her arm tighter. "We're going upstairs, now!"

"Cen, wait. We can't go without Wilt. I think he's in trouble." Carolyn pouted.

Her expression looked genuine, though I knew better than to believe her. She tricked me every time. "He's a grown-up. He can fend for himself." It seemed inappropriate that my aunt, who was supposedly in mourning, should be so flippant with her witchcraft by changing into Carolyn and attracting all sorts of unwanted attention.

Carolyn shook her head. "Uh-uh. He's a compulsive gambler. I should never have brought him here."

"You never should have done a lot of things," I scolded my aunt. "Like bringing me here against my will."

A slight smile played across Carolyn's lips. "You just need to have a little fun. Just let me find Wilt first. Then we'll go upstairs."

* * *

MINUTES later we found Wilt at a high stakes poker table. Even from twenty feet away, it was obvious that he was in trouble. His normally pallid complexion was bright red and he was sweating profusely. "He doesn't exactly have a poker face, does he?"

"Doesn't matter. All you need is a good hand." Carolyn dismissed me with a wave. "Mind your own business and let Wilt have a little fun."

Fun wasn't anything close to what Wilt was experiencing, though he brightened considerably when he spotted Carolyn. I was immediately suspicious. "You were helping Wilt win, weren't you?"

"Maybe for a while." Carolyn flashed both a smile and a little leg for the benefit of the three other men at Wilt's table. They leered in return. "I had them all so distracted, it just seemed like a wasted opportunity not to."

"You know that's not right, Aunt Pearl." I shook my head. "It's against WICCA rules to use magic to make money." The rules were particularly strict about using magic for personal enrichment. Conjuring up money was strictly forbidden. While I wasn't aware of any specific rules on gambling, I was pretty sure the same rules applied. Aunt Pearl wasn't exactly printing banknotes, but what she was doing was awfully close.

My aunt rolled her eyes. "I know the rules, Cen. Who said I used magic? I didn't need any. Just simple arithmetic."

"You counted cards?" The casino probably had cameras everywhere. Knowing my aunt, she had probably done it blatantly.

"Something like that." Carolyn inched closer to the table where she immediately caught the attention of a heavy-set man. His thick gold bracelet dug into his fleshy wrist as he fanned his cards, a swarthy caricature straight out of a mobster movie. His smug expression was either a bluff or a dead giveaway that his hand would trump Wilt's. His other hand rested on his thigh, close to his gun holster.

"It's kind of fun to pull one over on these wise guys. They think they're smarter than everyone else. You should try it sometime." Carolyn tossed back her blonde hair with an exaggerated flourish as she strutted around the table.

Counting cards was bad enough, but checking out Wilt's opponent's hand was cheating of the worst kind. I grabbed Carolyn's arm and pulled her back towards where I stood a few feet behind Wilt. "It's not going to be fun for long. Wilt can't afford to gamble like this with a minimum-wage job." I met her gaze as Wilt pushed a stack of fifty-dollar chips towards the table center. I lowered my voice. "He's in serious trouble."

I knew very little about poker, but even I saw that he had a terrible hand. He had no face cards, and not even so much as a pair of low-numbered cards. He was a terrible bluffer with no hope in hell of winning. Whether he was spending his own money, or part of Aunt Pearl's lottery winnings, the money wouldn't last long.

Carolyn ignored me.

I stepped closer to the table. "Wilt, finish your hand and let's go."

He turned for a split second, just long enough to glare at me. "Leave me alone. You're throwing off my concentration."

Aunt Pearl—still in her Carolyn Conroe disguise—swore under her breath. "You heard him. Mind your own business, Cendrine."

I gritted my teeth. "Focus, Aunt Pearl. Remember why we're here."

"You two know each other?" Wilt's brows arched in surprise.

I nodded, annoyed at having to cover for my aunt's dual identity.

"Small world." Wilt turned back to the table and his pathetic poker hand.

"Smaller than you might think." While I was relieved that Wilt had no idea that Carolyn was really Aunt Pearl—and a witch—her deceptive ways bothered me. Wilt was obviously attracted to Aunt Pearl's alter-ego, and Carolyn led him to think the feeling was mutual.

I turned back to Carolyn. "I'm doing it for his own good, Aunt Pearl."

"Sssh—don't call me that."

"You said he had a gambling problem."

"Did I? I don't remember that."

"You of all people should know better." I sucked in my breath as the players around the table matched and raised Wilt's bet. Arguing was pointless. It just prolonged the horrible train wreck unfolding before us.

Carolyn walked up behind Wilt and placed a hand on his shoulder.

Wilt glanced back at her and smiled, clearly enamored. He was even showing off a bit for his new love interest, which made his card playing all the more reckless. It was obvious Wilt had never had much female interest, let alone from a stunner like Carolyn. He basked in the attention from Carolyn and his envious poker opponents.

Carolyn had caught the attention of the other three men at the table, who leered in her general direction.

"I call," Mobster Guy dropped his cards on the table and grinned.

A Full House, three aces, and a pair of tens.

I grabbed Carolyn by the arm. "Wilt's getting annihilated. Make him stop, now." I couldn't watch any more of the slow-motion train wreck that was unfolding before my eyes.

"You want me to interrupt before he has a chance to win back his money?" She fluttered her fake eyelashes at me in mock innocence.

"You know I do."

She shrugged and caught the eye of the dealer and winked.

He smiled back, captivated.

Before I could say another word, everyone at the table was entranced.

Literally.

Carolyn Conroe had placed them all under a rewind spell. A split second later, the same scene played out before us. Only this time, Wilt had a pair of aces.

"Aunt Pearl!" I grabbed her arm. "That's worse than card count-ing! Change everything back to how it was before."

"No can do, missy. You weren't complaining earlier when you begged me to help you with a spell."

"But my spell was just to get me back home. It wouldn't financially ruin anyone."

"Anybody who gambles takes their own chances."

I crossed my arms. "What you're doing isn't right. Change everything back right now or I'll report you to WICCA. You know the rules." Cheating was grounds for immediate lifetime expulsion. No self-respecting witch would risk losing her powers.

"You'd betray your own aunt?" Carolyn crossed her arms and snorted. "For what? This is not cheating, Cen. I only moved Wilt back to an earlier point in time. Both of his choices were made of his own free will."

"But he chose differently this time," I protested. "He was dealt different cards."

"That's just the odds."

"You can't just rewind life over and over until you get the results you want," I said. "It doesn't work that way."

"You're wrong, Cen. That's exactly how life works."

ilt rose from the table and gathered up his chips. Aunt Pearl and I followed behind as he headed towards the exit and the hotel lobby. I felt a lot of eyes on us. Or rather on Carolyn, as she flashed leg and cleavage with every step. We only made it twenty feet before Wilt stopped, mesmerized by a bank of slot machines. He seemed completely oblivious to us. It was as if he was in a trance.

"Wilt." I stepped in front of him but his glassy eyes looked beyond me to the machines. He fished casino tokens from his pocket and sat down at the first machine.

One by one he dropped tokens into the machine.

"Stop him, Aunt Pearl! Wilt can't afford this." A half dozen drunken men in their mid-twenties had followed us from the casino. They stood ten feet away, whispering as they gawked at us. Judging from their ridiculous Hawaiian shirts and straw hats, they were part of a bachelor party.

"He can't afford it, but I sure can," Aunt Pearl said. "He's playing on my tab."

I shook my head. "Doesn't matter who pays. You're just making his gambling addiction worse." I couldn't see how her lottery win justified ruining a man's life.

Our fan club closed in around us in a semi-circle. From what I gathered from their drunken whispers, they were formulating a plan to introduce themselves. I turned back to Carolyn.

"You haven't even cashed in your ticket yet," I protested. "What if you made a mistake writing the numbers down?" It also dawned on me that if she hadn't cashed her ticket, she had to be getting the money from somewhere else. I was afraid to ask where. She wasn't anywhere near wealthy enough to finance a gambling junket.

"The ticket's good. I used that validation machine thing, so I'm sure. What could possibly go wrong?" She waved her hand in a flourish, almost swatting the groom, who seemed oblivious as his hat flew off.

"Plenty," I said. "Maybe there's a mistake with the numbers. What if you lose the ticket? I hope you put it somewhere safe."

Carolyn reached into her cleavage, which attracted a few whistles from her admirers. Her eyes widened and she broke out into a sweat.

"What's wrong?"

Her hand flew to her mouth. "It was there a few minutes ago. Oh my gawd! I lost the ticket!"

My stomach churned as I thought of the RV, the gambling tab, and who knew what else Aunt Pearl had bought on credit. "At least we have the rest of Wilt's gambling chips."

I grabbed Wilt's arm just as he dumped his last handful of tokens into the slot machine and pulled the handle.

Too late. I swore under my breath.

Carolyn Conroe erupted into peals of laughter as she patted my back. "Calm down, Cen. I was just kidding."

The bachelor party men gawked as Carolyn adjusted her cleavage and gave her bosom a final tap. She grinned at the stag party men. "Still got it."

I steered Wilt away from the slot machine.

"That's my lucky machine! It's about to pay off." Wilt yanked his arm from my grasp.

"It'll never pay off," I said. "Let's quit while we're ahead."

Wilt shook his head. "The first time in a long time I'm winning, and you want me to quit?"

"You weren't winning anything," I said. "You just used all your chips."

"Temporary setback," Wilt protested.

I glanced at Carolyn, but she was too busy to notice. The bachelor party men surrounded her, each competing for her attention. She was soaking up every minute of it.

I still had one advantage. Wilt didn't know that Carolyn was really Aunt Pearl.

I lowered my voice so Carolyn couldn't hear. "Wilt, I need your help. Aunt Pearl is missing and I need to find her. Aren't you supposed to be her personal chauffeur and bodyguard?"

Wilt paled. "Uh, yeah. Oh my god. I'd better find her."

It seemed a bit of an overreaction, but at least Wilt took his job seriously.

"I know you're just letting off a little steam after a long drive here, but we urgently need to find her. She needs her medication." If anyone needed meds right now it was me, but Wilt bought my little white lie.

His mouth dropped open. "I screwed up, didn't I? Sorry, I don't know what's got into me."

"That's okay, Wilt." I stepped away from the slot machine and motioned for him to follow. One of the bachelors jostled us, annoyed at losing his position close to Carolyn.

Wilt followed, looking contrite. "I got caught up in the cards instead of watching out for Miss Pearl. I can't help it, Cendrine. All the flashy lights and noises intoxicate me. It makes me feel like I'm on drugs or something."

"Don't worry about it. You go upstairs to the suite and see if you can find anything. I'll look around here." I had no intention of doing that, but I needed Wilt out of the casino. I also had to get Carolyn alone and convince her to change back into Aunt Pearl. Carolyn Conroe attracted way too much male attention.

Wilt nodded and turned to leave. He made it only about ten feet when a large burly man blocked his way.

My heart jumped as I recognized the man as Mobster Guy, the burly poker player from moments earlier.

CHAPTER 29

"Why'd you leave the table? We were just getting to know each other." Mobster Guy clamped a fleshy hand down on Wilt's shoulder. "We've got a little problem, you and I."

"I'm done playing." Wilt shook as he spoke. "I paid all my bets, so I don't see what the problem is."

"You don't see counting cards as a problem?" The man tightened his grip. "You don't fool me one bit. Your losing hand at the end was just to make it look real."

"That doesn't make any sense," I protested. "He lost a lot at the end." I debated whether I should go find Rocco. Then I remembered the lobby shootout and decided against it. These family rivalries tended to turn deadly.

Mobster Guy glared at me so hard I thought his eyes would explode out of his head. "Nobody asked you, honey."

Wilt winced in pain as Mobster Guy dug deeper.

"I see what you and your friend are up to." The man nodded towards Carolyn. "She's your distraction, isn't she? She sidetracks the rest of us till we're not paying any attention to the game."

"Nope. I won fair and square." Wilt wrenched his shoulder from the man's grip. "I gotta go."

"You ain't going anywhere. You owe me big time." Mobster guy grabbed Wilt's collar and yanked it so hard upwards that Wilt almost came out the other end. He was twice the size of Wilt, almost three hundred pounds, with an outsized temper to match.

Wilt shook his head. "I don't owe nobody nothin'. Not even the time of day."

Wilt's flippant response was about to get us into a whole mess of trouble. I tugged on his arm. "Wilt, let's go."

Mobster guy pulled Wilt in the other direction, ripping his shirt seam. A button popped off Wilt's shirt and landed on the plush casino carpet.

Mobster guy's face flushed an angry red, a sore loser.

"Carolyn," I yelled. "Get over here."

To my surprise, Carolyn immediately extricated herself from her admirers. "What's all the fuss about?"

"We need help," I whispered. "Now would be a good time to rewind."

"Oh dear," Carolyn frowned. "Wilt really is in trouble. That's Jimmy, Manny La Manna's right-hand man. He's got a hair-trigger temper. Wilt sure knows how to pick his enemies."

"You didn't recognize him earlier? He's been playing cards with Wilt the whole time you were counting them. How could you miss him?"

"He looks a lot different since I last saw him. He's gained a lot of weight. Besides, I was multi-tasking, Cen. Counting cards, counting men…it got a little confusing."

"Pay attention, Aunt Pearl. We have to undo this."

"Sssh—don't call me that. I'm Carolyn, remember?"

"Fine. Just get us out of this mess."

Carolyn stepped back and crossed her arms. "You talk to me like

that and expect favors, missy? Well, you're not getting my cooperation. You want another rewind spell? Go do it yourself."

"But I can't…"

"Just admit you were wrong and apologize."

A couple of Carolyn's admirers wandered over to see what the
fuss was about. I didn't want a brawl but didn't see why I had to
apologize. I hadn't done anything wrong.

Jimmy's fleshy arms wrapped around Wilt's neck in a choke
hold.

Wilt's arms flailed at his sides as he tried to escape Jimmy's
clutches.

"Aunt Pearl, please—just forget about me. Do it for Wilt."

"Stop using my real name!" Her eyes narrowed. "Are you sorry or
not?"

"Okay, fine. I'm sorry. Just reverse the spell and take Wilt out of
his misery!" I couldn't bear to watch another second. Wilt's eyes
bulged from Jimmy's vice grip. He looked like an insect about to be
squashed.

"I really wish you'd practice your own magic and not rely on me
all the time." Carolyn muttered under her breath. "If only you would
apply yourself."

I rolled my eyes. It was too late to do anything about that now,
but for once I agreed with Aunt Pearl. As soon as I got back to Westwick Corners, I resolved to return to my lessons, if only to counteract Aunt Pearl's irresponsibility.

Aunt Pearl snapped her fingers. "One, two, three, make it not
to be…"

My gasp echoed throughout the entire casino. The cavernous
space became eerily silent, with no voices or clanging slot machines.
Hundreds of gamblers at slot machines and tables were all frozen in
various states of suspended animation.

"Uh-oh." Carolyn's mirth from moments ago had been replaced
by worry.

"What is it?" I glanced up at the ceiling, wondering if the rewind spell affected anyone elsewhere in the building, such as the security employees watching the casino floor by camera. Aunt Pearl's witchcraft was recorded for posterity if anyone happened to review the surveillance footage. I was certain that was done in the casino on a very regular basis.

Carolyn grimaced as she tried to pry Jimmy's fingers from Wilt's neck. "It's not working. I stopped the spell at the wrong moment, and now I don't know what to do."

"Can't you just rewind a few seconds earlier?" It seemed so obvious, I wondered why she was even mentioning it.

"Uh-uh. I can't do unwind and rewind precise enough to stop within a fraction of a second. Even if I'm fast enough, it might jeopardize Wilt's safety."

"Well, we can't let Jimmy strangle Wilt." I stepped toward the two men to get a closer look. "Give me your shoe."

"It's not that bad, is it?" Carolyn tilted her head as she studied the two men. Wilt's face was frozen in terror and his hands clutched Jimmy's in a death grip.

"Just give me your shoe, quick!"

Carolyn reluctantly handed over her stiletto. I wedged the spiked heel under Jimmy's fingers and slowly pulled until they loosened from Wilt's neck. Then I leaned back and pulled as hard as I could. Jimmy's knuckles cracked as his fingers unwrapped and he pulled away from Wilt. I immediately lost my balance and fell backward onto the carpeted casino floor.

A split second later, Jimmy fell on top of me and everything went black.

CHAPTER 30

I rose to a sitting position to find Wilt and Carolyn staring down at me with looks of concern. "Where's Jimmy?" I gasped for breath as my ribcage slowly expanded. I felt like a flattened pancake after being squashed under Jimmy's weight.

"Gone," Carolyn pointed towards the door as she held out her hand. She had already put her shoe back on. "Get up. We've got no time to waste."

I did as I was told, but I was confused. I also had a pounding headache. I stood opposite Carolyn and scanned the casino floor. People milled around machines and tables, placing their bets as if nothing had happened. "What's the rush?"

Carolyn frowned. "Jimmy's going to tell Manny, and when Manny comes after Wilt he'll find out that I had something to do with it. There's going to be trouble."

My mouth dropped open. "Manny knows you're a witch?"

"Of course he knows, Cen."

"I thought you said he was just a casual fling?" He had to mean more to her than that if he knew about Aunt Pearl's supernatural talents. "Exactly how serious is your relationship?"

"I don't kiss and tell, and I'm certainly not going to share the lurid details of my love life with my niece." She placed her hands on her hips. "It's none of your business."

"You pissed off a mobster. You just made it my business."

Carolyn waved me off. "No time for that now. We better make ourselves scarce."

Wilt walked zombie-like towards a nearby slot machine. He rummaged in his pockets, finally turning them inside out, empty. Carolyn beckoned him over and he fell in behind us. We headed out of the casino and towards the hotel lobby.

The lobby bustled with hotel guests, most of whom probably had no clue about the earlier gunfire.

"I'm not letting up until you tell me more about your relationship with Manny. Was this before or after he married Carla?" I felt underdressed beside Carolyn, though my casual dress matched just about everyone else in the lobby.

"Before, but I don't see why that matters. We met at one of Carla's parties, back when she still lived in Westwick Corners. Manny was in town for a few days on business. He was immediately attracted to me." Carolyn smiled and ran her fingers through her long blonde hair.

"Attracted to Pearl, or attracted to Carolyn?"

"What does that matter?"

"It matters a lot. Does he know about your Carolyn act?"

"Uh-huh. He knows everything. And don't call it that," Carolyn sniffed. "Carolyn is very real to me. I can assure you she is very real to a lot of people around here. Including Manny. He thinks it's kind of sexy."

I covered my ears. "Too much information." I didn't want to imagine my elderly aunt—even in her Carolyn alter ego—getting intimate with a member of the opposite sex.

I turned and saw that two of the bachelor party men still followed us, hovering back a few feet. "I know you're flattered by all the attention, but this is getting creepy. It's like they're stalking us."

Wilt snapped to attention and marched towards the men. "I'll take care of them."

Carolyn waited until he was out of earshot and leaned closer. "At least they'll keep Wilt occupied for a while." She winked at the two men and followed me to the elevators.

I rolled my eyes, pressed the elevator button, and prayed for the doors to open before either Wilt or Carolyn found any more trouble.

My prayers were answered as the elevator doors opened and I stepped into the empty elevator.

Carolyn followed me in. "Jimmy was card-counting too. That's why he was so furious. He wasn't supposed to have any competition at the table. Manny will think I helped Wilt."

"You did help him." My mouth dropped open as the larger implications of Carolyn's statement sunk in. "Wait a minute. Are you saying that Jimmy was card counting with the casino's knowledge?" That implied that Rocco was involved somehow.

"The casino has to know. They monitor everything, so how could they not know?" Carolyn dropped her head and muttered to herself.

"Hey, wait for me!" Wilt jumped in the elevator just as the doors closed behind him. Whatever he had said to our admirers had worked, because they were gone.

"How is witchcraft worse than counting cards? Either way is cheating." As far as I could see, Jimmy had been beaten at his own game and was a sore loser. I didn't see what it had to do with Manny, or why witchcraft was worse than counting cards. Both were forms of cheating in my eyes.

"Maybe, but Manny doesn't see it that way. Card counting is how Manny and his guys make some of their money. Any witchcraft that undermines his business is something he won't tolerate."

"The card-counting seems awfully labor intensive. Jimmy would have to win a lot to make it worthwhile." I wondered if Rocco knew what was going on at his own casino.

Carolyn rolled her eyes. "They look for high rollers like Wilt appears to be."

"What are you guys talking about?" Wilt rubbed his forehead. "Who was card-counting?"

"Never mind, we'll talk about it later." I turned to Carolyn. "Manny won't know you were involved."

Carolyn shook her head. "The surveillance cameras. Anyone watching will see that everything here on the floor froze with my rewind spell. It's obviously magic."

"I doubt it. Most people would think the temporary freeze is a technical glitch with the camera or something."

"Except that not all of us were frozen," Carolyn said. "Don't you see? That in itself proves we are witches. Anyone reviewing the surveillance footage will see us moving around while everyone else is frozen in place."

"Oh," I said. "I hadn't thought of that. But that's okay. We'll just tell Rocco. He already knows we're witches, and he can just erase the footage."

"Hmmm." Carolyn frowned.

"What's wrong with that? Manny doesn't work at Rocco's casino, so he'd never see the footage anyways."

"I guess I forgot to mention that part." Carolyn paused and drew a deep breath. "Manny has already infiltrated the casino. A few of his men are now on security detail here. Now that Carla's gone, nothing is going to stop him from making his takeover official."

I stepped out of the elevator and trailed behind Carolyn and Wilt into the suite. After all the clanging and people downstairs, the stillness of the suite infused a strange sense of calm. I hated to admit it, but it was beginning to feel like home.

"We can't stay here. Let's pack up our things and leave." Carolyn headed for the stairs, but froze suddenly in her tracks. "Manny's people will be tracking our every move."

My mouth dropped open. Christophe sat beside Mom on the sofa, a bottle of beer in hand. It seemed strange to be drinking on the job, but maybe things worked differently in Vegas. Even stranger was his choice of beverage, given his penchant for mixing fancy drinks.

But it was the man sitting opposite Christophe in the armchair that caught my attention.

"Tyler! You're here!"

He grinned and rose to greet me. "When I didn't hear from you, I got worried. These crime families are dangerous, so I thought I'd better drop by. I caught a flight over."

As if it was the easiest thing in the world.

"How did you find us?" I rushed over and kissed him on the cheek.

He shrugged. "It wasn't that hard to figure out. Just go where the Racatellis are."

Carolyn shook her head, clearly not pleased to see Tyler. "Siding with the law. How could you, Cen? You've changed sides."

Tyler frowned. "Do I know you? You look sort of familiar."

"I don't think so," Carolyn stared after Wilt as he walked out onto the patio. "I'll be right back."

"I'm coming with you." I trailed behind Carolyn as she headed outside.

"We have to get out of here, Wilt." Carolyn beckoned him with a wave of her hand.

"I just met you." Wilt paused in the doorway. "You're pretty and all, but I barely know you. Why would you want to run away with me?"

Carolyn exhaled and threw her hands in the air. "Tell him, Cen."

"Tell him what?" I certainly wasn't about to explain that Carolyn was just a witchy disguise conjured up by Aunt Pearl. "You created this mess. You'll have to get yourself out of it."

Wilt shook his head slowly. "You two can argue as much as you want. I've got to get out of here before that guy comes looking for me. I'll just take off somewhere in the RV. Maybe I'll hide out in the desert."

"In a giant RV?" Carolyn snorted. "Yeah. Like nobody will notice that at all."

"You don't need to be sarcastic," Wilt said.

I caught up with them and grabbed Wilt's arm. "Are you crazy? You're no match for these thugs. Even if you leave Las Vegas, they'll probably come looking for you."

"Don't be ridiculous, Cen. Wilt can easily disappear for good."

"For good?" He suddenly looked doubtful. "I don't see how. I have nowhere to go. I'm no good at anything. I even lost Miss Pearl."

I glared at Carolyn. "Can't you do something?"

"You mean, like change back—"

"That's exactly what I mean." I turned to Wilt. "Promise me you'll stay right here until I come back. I think I might know where Aunt Pearl is."

Wilt looked doubtful.

"I can't help you unless you cooperate, Wilt."

"Do what she says," Carolyn added as she followed me back inside. She smiled indulgently. "Wilt needs a bit of fresh air, so we can just let him stew for a bit. I think he had a little too much to drink. Speaking of which, I could use a Cosmo, Chris. No one mixes them quite like you do."

Christophe frowned. "I've never made you a drink before."

I waved my hand in dismissal. "I might have mentioned you and your mixology skills to Carolyn." I glared at my aunt.

"A man of many talents." Tyler smiled. "At least you ladies have been in good hands with Christophe protecting you. Might be best to stay in the suite for the next few hours."

"No can do," Carolyn said. "We've got to get out of here."

Tyler's eyes narrowed. "You sure we haven't met before? I could swear I've seen you in Westwick Corners."

My pulse quickened as I steeled myself for Carolyn's response.

Carolyn batted her eyelashes. "West-what?"

"Never mind." Tyler turned to me. "Things are about to come to a head. Promise me you'll stay here in the suite?"

"We aren't going anywhere," I answered for both of us.

We headed upstairs and marched into the bedroom. "Change back into Pearl right now."

"Can't it wait?"

"No, Aunt Pearl. Do it now."

For once she listened to me.

I breathed a sigh of relief as glamorous Carolyn slowly faded and no-nonsense Aunt Pearl solidified before my eyes. She wore a white tennis outfit, not exactly her normal attire. The short skirt exposed slim, wrinkled legs with a touch of sun damage. "Good. Let's go downstairs and get Christophe to help Wilt."

"Do we really have to involve the police?"

I glared at her. "I don't think we have any choice."

"All right. Have it your way." Aunt Pearl hoisted a huge white duffel bag off the bed and onto her shoulder.

"We aren't going anywhere," I reminded her.

"I know, I know." She looked like she was heading out for a tennis match with her gear slung over her shoulder.

I followed behind my aunt as we descended the stairs.

"Sheriff Gates, what a surprise!"

"Going somewhere, Pearl?" Tyler asked.

Aunt Pearl shook her head. "Nope. Just getting my stuff ready for my tennis match tomorrow."

"That's good. I think we all need to stay inside for a while."

CHAPTER 32

Imprisonment in a luxury Vegas hotel suite wasn't so bad after all, now that Tyler was here. I wouldn't even mind prolonging our stay a little longer. I was really touched to know that he had traveled so many miles, just to make sure I was safe.

No man had ever done anything like that for me before.

Maybe we did stand a chance after all.

I smiled at him.

Tyler returned my smile. "It's wasn't that hard to track you down since I knew you were visiting Rocco Racatelli. I figured you'd show up at his hotel sooner or later."

Rocco.

Tyler.

I felt nothing for Rocco right now, but that was because he was nowhere near me. Would the attraction spell take over my free will again? I was worried about what that meant for Tyler and me.

"But how..." My eyes darted to Christophe and then back to Tyler. They had apparently already introduced themselves. A good thing, since I didn't know quite how to explain our strange butler to Tyler.

Tyler seemed to read my mind. "Christophe is a former colleague of mine. His sole reason for being in this suite is for your protection."

"You were a mobster too, Sheriff Gates? Never would have guessed." Mom's eyes widened in shock as she slid to the opposite end of the sofa, away from Christophe. She looked to me for reassurance.

"He's fine. Mom." Mom's reaction seemed over the top, especially considering her bad boyfriend choices.

Tyler laughed. "Don't worry, Ruby. Christophe and I worked together as undercover cops. Before I came to Westwick Corners, I worked here in Vegas."

"I knew you were too good to be true." Aunt Pearl paled as she eyed Christophe. "But you make such great martinis. What a crying shame."

Christophe smiled. "What can I say? I'm a man of many talents."

"Why do we need protection?" I knew exactly why, but wanted a straight answer from Christophe. If the police considered Carla's death accidental, Christophe's presence made no sense.

"Nothing you need to know at the moment," Christophe said.

"How did you even know that we would be here?" I asked. "What about Rocco? He's the one that really needs protection right now." I wanted answers, but I wasn't getting very far.

"Don't worry about him. He's covered. We've taken care of everything. Now let me do my job and you'll all be fine," Christophe said.

"We don't need protection," Aunt Pearl protested. "We're perfectly capable of taking care of ourselves."

I grabbed Aunt Pearl and pulled her into the kitchen. "Here's our chance to get justice for Carla. We need to show that autopsy report to Christophe."

"We can't do that. He's probably just as crooked as the rest of them. They're convinced that Carla's death was an accident, so I don't want to make waves. There's not much I can do about their incompetence."

"Of all people, I thought you would try harder to get justice for your friend. You accuse me of not applying myself with my magic. Well, you don't put much effort into real life." I shook my head. "I thought Carla was your friend. Don't you care about her?"

"Of course I do. But there are other ways to see justice served."

"None of your ideas have worked so far. In fact, you just get us into more and more trouble. And poor Wilt now has to run for his life, all because you mixed him up in your crazy card-counting scheme. You need to stop your witchy antics right now, before you screw up whatever it is the police are actually investigating." I still wasn't clear on what that was and hoped to get some information from Tyler.

"Give me the autopsy report." I held out my hand.

Aunt Pearl backed away, her palms outstretched. "I seemed to have misplaced it."

"You better find it. Unless that autopsy report was something you just made up."

Aunt Pearl's eyes moistened with tears. "Of course not. I would never fabricate something like that. That would be horrible."

"I'll give you one chance to make things right, Aunt Pearl." I pointed towards the living room. "On the other side of that door are two people that can help. Will you give them proof that Carla was strangled, or are you going to hide what you know?"

"Okay, fine. We'll do it your way." She shooed me towards the kitchen door and pushed me through it. "We've got no time to waste. Jimmy's going to come after us."

"I'll get Wilt." I brushed past her and headed to the patio to get Wilt. I opened the patio doors and stepped outside. I circled the deck but found no sign of him. I broke into a run as I retraced my steps, checking and rechecking every corner and alcove of the wraparound deck. I leaned over the railing and looked down onto the street far below, where specks of people milled around the hotel entrance.

Wilt had disappeared without a trace.

I ran towards the doors and almost ran into Aunt Pearl. "He's gone."

Aunt Pearl's bottom lip trembled. "How can that be?"

"You helped him, didn't you? Because there's no possible way he left the 26th floor of this hotel unless magic was involved."

"Maybe." Aunt Pearl's eyes darted back and forth.

"Running away doesn't solve anything, Aunt Pearl. In fact, it makes things worse for Wilt. He's on his own, and he's not even thinking clearly. Find him, Aunt Pearl."

Wilt was far too sloppy and disorganized to pull off any crime, let alone murder. He couldn't even follow Aunt Pearl's convoluted card-counting scheme.

But maybe that wasn't Wilt's fault after all. I flashed back to Wilt's comments in the elevator. He had seemed completely oblivious to the card counting. Aunt Pearl's claims had so many inconsistencies that I just didn't know where to start. "Let's go inside and tell them."

Aunt Pearl crossed her arms. "No."

"Wilt might evade the police, but he can't run from the La Manna organization forever. Wherever he goes, they will find him and retaliate. Then it will be too late. At least with the police, he will be protected in custody."

For the first time, Aunt Pearl wavered. "I guess you're right. They'll track him down and I can't protect him with my magic forever."

"Good. It's settled." I clamped my hand around her bony arm and steered her towards the door. "I want you to tell Christophe and Tyler everything."

"You sure? Everything?"

"Leave out the witchy parts, of course. Tell them everything else, including the romantic relationships and Carla's marriages, sham or otherwise."

I stepped inside and announced the news. "Wilt's gone."

"That's impossible. He would have had to walk right past us. And he couldn't jump that many stories and survive." Mom's hand flew to her mouth as she grasped what had really happened.

Aunt Pearl coughed.

"You didn't," Mom whispered as she squeezed her sister's arm. "You helped him, didn't you?"

"Ouch!" Aunt Pearl slapped Mom's arm. "I had to do something. Otherwise, Wilt's as good as dead once Manny gets his hands on him."

Tyler's mouth dropped open. "You helped Wilt escape? But he was just outside…"

Tyler's comment struck me as odd, since he couldn't possibly know what had just transpired down in the casino. "We'll find him. We can discuss details later, but Aunt Pearl has more pressing news for you. Right, Aunt Pearl?"

"Uh-huh," she muttered.

"Speak up, Pearl," Tyler said. "And don't spare any details. These are ruthless people we're dealing with."

I broke out into a sweat. "Tell them about Manny's men and how they've infiltrated the hotel's security. Since Wilt's escape will show on the surveillance footage, he's doomed."

Aunt Pearl nodded. "It might already be too late."

Aunt Pearl headed towards the foyer, her duffel bag still slung over her shoulder. "I know where to find Wilt."

"No, Pearl," Tyler said. "You're not going anywhere."

Aunt Pearl glared at him but returned to the living room.

Christophe walked over to the patio doors. He spoke in a low voice into his cell phone. Less than a minute later, he returned to the sofa. "I'm confident that we'll find Wilt pretty quick. But innocent people normally don't disappear like that. What's he running from?"

"Manny, of course," Aunt Pearl said.

"I doubt that's it," said Christophe. "He's got police protection in a secure suite. Now, why would he go outside to face Manny, unless there was something else going on?"

"I can't take this anymore! Of course there's something else going on. Only you people are too dumb to see it. It's the key to everything that's happened." Aunt Pearl squeezed her head with her hands. "You can't figure it out, so I might as well tell you. Danny killed Carla. Wilt witnessed the whole thing."

"Danny "Bones" Battilana? That's impossible because he was

already dead. I mean, we even saw him at the funeral." Christophe looked pointedly at me and cleared his throat.

"That doesn't mean he died before Carla," I said.

Christophe shook his head. "Of course it does. He was already in the bottom of her casket. Besides, her death was ruled an accident."

"Well, I have it on good authority that it's not the way things went down." Aunt Pearl crossed her arms defiantly.

"I don't see how. All of you arrived after Carla's death, including Wilt. How could he have possibly witnessed Carla's death?" Christophe frowned.

I flashed back to the coffin fiasco. "There's still one thing that's bothering me. At the funeral, Bones just looked so...so..." I struggled for the right words.

"Like he was past his best-before date?" Mom asked.

"Yes," I said. "Judging by the condition of his body, he was probably dead before Carla."

"No, that's not the case," Aunt Pearl said. "Carla got embalmed, but Danny didn't. That's why he looked so bad. Besides, any embalmer worth his salt would have camouflaged the bullet hole in Bones' forehead."

Christophe's eyes narrowed. "You seem to know a lot."

Aunt Pearl shook her head. "Not really. I'm just very observant."

"Well, one thing's obvious. Rocco would never have hidden Danny inside his grandmother's coffin," Mom said.

"Don't be so sure," Christophe said. "People do desperate things to cover their tracks."

"Can we get back on topic here?" Aunt Pearl scowled. "Wilt called me right after it happened."

"But when? We didn't leave for Vegas till after—"

"There's such a thing as telephones and email, Cen."

My aunt was notoriously bad with technology, so I doubted she had used either. Any communication would have been done in person. "When were you last in Vegas?"

Aunt Pearl's eyes narrowed. "A while ago."

"When, exactly?" Christophe jotted notes on a small pad of paper he had pulled from his shirt pocket.

"A couple of days ago."

Mom gasped. "Before Carla died? Why didn't you mention any of this before?"

"You never asked." Aunt Pearl glared at Mom. "Oh, and another thing. Nobody asked you for your opinion. All of your guessing is just confusing things."

Mom visibly wilted.

"Carla summoned me here. She said it was top secret, but when I arrived here, she was gone."

"As in dead, gone?" Mom asked.

"Of course as in dead." Aunt Pearl paced back and forth in front of the patio doors. "I found her in the pool. It pains me to think that she died just a few feet away from us."

"She died here?" Mom shot out of her seat. "I thought Carla died at her home."

"This hotel suite was her home," Aunt Pearl said.

"But…I was in that pool." Mom's voice broke.

Christophe looked away, clearly uncomfortable.

"The police ruled her death an accident without even looking around," Aunt Pearl said. "Case closed. The local police are either incompetent or bought and paid for."

Tyler bristled. "Don't go making accusations without proof, Pearl. This is my old job, and I know most of them. No cop I know would cover up a murder."

I hated to side with Aunt Pearl, but she had a point. "There was something odd about how they found Carla, face-up in her pool. Drowning victims are almost always face-down."

That got both Christophe's and Tyler's attention. Christophe scribbled a note.

The last thing we needed was for Tyler and Aunt Pearl to go

head to head.

Mom's hand flew to her mouth. "How could you not tell me any of this? You let me go in the pool."

Pearl dismissed her sister with a wave. "This is exactly why I didn't say anything. You always overreact."

"Maybe Carla fell just like Mom did. Only her accident was fatal." I said it more to encourage Aunt Pearl, who seemed reluctant to reveal the details. We couldn't waste any more time getting to the bottom of things.

"No. Carla was strangled." Aunt Pearl pulled the autopsy report from her pocket and handed it to Christophe. "The medical examiner said so, right here in this report."

"Where did you get this?" Christophe frowned.

"Never mind," Aunt Pearl snapped. "You want to read it or not?"

Christophe didn't answer. He traced his finger along the report as he read it. "No water in the lungs. That is odd."

"Now do you believe me?" Aunt Pearl's eyes moistened with tears.

"I don't know what to make of this," Christophe said. "Bones is already dead. I happen to know the medical examiner fairly well and she's above reproach. My source told me that she had called it a tragic accident. I can't imagine her withholding information or doctoring a report."

"Well, I guess your 'source' lied." Aunt Pearl made quotation marks with her fingers. "The medical examiner and Wilt are the only ones who know the truth. And Wilt's the sole witness to Carla's murder. That's the real reason he's on the run."

"You better help us find him, Pearl," Tyler said. "It may already be too late."

CHAPTER 34

Manny and his cronies were already under surveillance, and Christophe put out an all-points bulletin for Wilt. I suspected he wouldn't remain missing for long, especially traveling in the massive RV. I felt a faint glimmer of hope that Wilt might survive after all.

"If Wilt's account is true, then I guess the husband really did do it," Tyler said. "That's how it happens almost all of the time."

"We'll get Wilt's statement when we find him." Christophe turned to Aunt Pearl. "In the meantime, tell me everything you know."

Aunt Pearl held up her hands, palms outward. "There's nothing else—"

"The fake wedding," I prompted.

"Oh, that." Aunt Pearl glared at me. "Bones pretended to be the grieving husband, but he was only ever after one thing: the Racatelli empire. He forced Carla to marry him. If she didn't, he threatened to kill Rocco. She agreed, but she outsmarted him. All the wedding paperwork was fake. The marriage license, the ceremony, everything."

I flashed back to Rocco's claim that Carla had a pre-nup. It apparently wasn't the case—just Carla's way of appeasing Rocco so that he didn't feel threatened. "Bones thought that by killing Carla, he would inherit the Racatelli estate. He would cut Rocco out, at least financially."

Mom sighed in relief. "Thank goodness the wedding was fake. It means that Rocco's inheritance is safe after all. At least from Bones."

Aunt Pearl raised her hand. "What about Manny La Manna's people in the hotel? He's already got his people inside the hotel, trying to take over. He's infiltrated the casino operations."

Aunt Pearl then turned to Christophe. "Is that why you're here? Because of Manny's attempted takeover?"

"I can't answer that, Pearl. All I can tell you is that you're safe as long as you stay here."

"The rivalry between the Racatelli, Battilana, and La Manna families has been underway for a long time now," Tyler said. "It's not exactly a secret. The lobby shootout was one of those flare-ups."

Aunt Pearl shook her head. "Such a shame. Manny was Carla's one true love. They had a really good thing going."

I frowned, thinking Aunt Pearl was with Manny. "B-but you…"

"I told you Manny was just a fling for me," she snapped. "When Carla told me about her feelings for him, I dumped him immediately. I didn't approve of her choice of husband, but who am I to stand in the way of her happiness?"

I gasped. "She married Manny too? For real?"

Aunt Pearl nodded. "That marriage was the real thing. In fact, it happened just hours before she died. It was a secret wedding, and I was one of only two witnesses. Rocco was the other."

Now things were beginning to make sense. "The shootout wasn't really about the Racatelli empire, was it? This is about the wedding. Rocco didn't like it, and Manny wasn't going to let Rocco get in the way. I guess Manny got what he wanted after all."

Aunt Pearl started to cry. "I did everything I could, but it wasn't enough in the end."

I had seen my aunt close to tears many times, a lot of them in the last twenty-four hours. But I had never seen her cry. I placed an arm around her shoulder and hugged her. "It's okay. You did your best. I just wish you had told us the truth to begin with. It would have made it a lot easier on everyone."

We both jumped as Christophe's cell phone rang.

He stood and walked towards the kitchen. He spoke in a low voice, but judging from his body language it appeared to be good news.

"They're on Wilt's trail, and not a moment too soon. Manny's thugs are following him. I'm hoping we get to him first."

Mom shivered.

"There are a few things we should take care of, Aunt Pearl. Like gathering up Carla's documents. The marriage certificates for starters. That will back up your account."

Mom stood, still a little unsteady on her feet. "I'll help."

It took us less than ten minutes to find the documents in Carla's desk drawer. "These look genuine to me." I pointed to the marriage certificate for Danny and Carla as I handed the papers to Tyler.

"I don't see why this wouldn't be real," he said. "Carla and Bones had a valid license, and the ceremony was witnessed by both Rocco and the hotel manager. Where's the fake part?"

Aunt Pearl blanched. "The marriage licence—I thought it was faked."

"Uh-uh," Tyler said. "It's from the wedding chapel down the street. Their marriage was real, all right."

Christophe frowned. "There's just one question, and I think I already know the answer. Who killed Bones?"

If Christophe and Tyler were annoyed by Aunt Pearl's ever-changing story, they didn't let on.

"We need to get the story straight from Wilt," Christophe said. "Maybe he's more than a witness."

Tyler nodded. "Maybe he killed Carla. He doesn't have an alibi, and he was the last one to see Carla alive." Tyler turned to Aunt Pearl. "At least, according to Pearl's version of events."

"What's that supposed to mean?" Aunt Pearl frowned.

Tyler didn't respond.

"We'll find out soon enough." Christophe dropped his phone on the table. "They've got Wilt. He's safe."

"What a relief," Mom said.

"I already told you. Wilt didn't do it." Aunt Pearl stomped her foot in frustration. "Bones killed Carla, thinking that as her surviving spouse, he would inherit everything."

"Maybe Rocco put Bones up to it, and then killed Bones after," Tyler said. "With Bones, Carla's husband gone, Rocco gets everything."

"That's even more ridiculous," Aunt Pearl snapped. "Stop guessing and face the facts."

"Maybe Manny La Manna killed Carla," I said.

"Manny would never do such a thing." Aunt Pearl seemed offended by my suggestion.

"You think these guys have morals?" I asked.

Aunt Pearl glared at me.

"How come you know so much about these people?" Christophe scratched his chin. "Speaking of which, how did you know that Manny had infiltrated the hotel, Pearl? You seem to know an awful lot for an innocent bystander."

Shivers ran down my spine as I flashed back to the funeral, where Christophe had seemed so friendly with Manny. If Tyler trusted him, then he had to be all right, but I still felt uneasy. "Tell him, Aunt Pearl."

"I want immunity from prosecution first."

"It doesn't work like it does on TV, Pearl." Christophe smiled. "Besides, I don't have the authority to do that. Only the District Attorney can make deals like that. I can, however, take you downtown for a very long interrogation."

Silence.

"Or, you can cooperate and we can get the formalities over with." Christophe smiled. "I know which one I would choose."

"Fine." Aunt Pearl frowned and slumped down on the couch.

Luckily Christophe wasn't interested in the details of how Wilt got away, only in finding him. He pulled out his ringing cell phone and spoke into it. "Fine. See you in ten."

Christophe turned back to Aunt Pearl. "They'll have Wilt back here in a few minutes. In the meantime I want you to tell me everything you know about Manny. I'm all ears. You can start talking now."

* * *

AUNT PEARL FINISHED her account ten minutes later, omitting the romantic entanglements. That hardly surprised me, since her accounts were at odds with Mom's version. One of them was lying, and I had no doubt who.

Aunt Pearl was surprisingly open with Christophe about Manny and the security infiltration. She also volunteered additional information about the Racatelli, Battilana, and La Manna crime organizations that even Christophe seemed unaware of.

At least, he acted as if he was surprised. That's probably all that it was—an act. He was a surprisingly good actor, which, of course, a good undercover agent had to be. All of us had fallen hook, line, and sinker for his butler cover.

"It's all my fault." Aunt Pearl sniffed. "I was just trying to help Wilt. I promised Carla that I would take care of him if anything ever happened to her."

Mom gasped. "You knew Wilt before he came to Westwick Corners?"

Aunt Pearl nodded. "He came to me for help. All I did was help him get away."

I raised my brows.

"Okay, so maybe a little gambling on the side. This is Vegas, after all."

"Go on." Christophe pulled out his phone again. "Okay if I record all this?"

Aunt Pearl nodded.

"Who was Wilt running from?" I answered my own question. "Bones? Does his murder have something to do with Wilt?"

Aunt Pearl nodded slowly. "Sort of."

"What do you mean, sort of?"

"Wilt had a big gambling debt. When he found out that his loan had ultimately come from Bones, he was mortified. He thought Bones wanted to kill him. But Bones would never do that, if only because it didn't make good business sense. Dead men never pay off their debts, but scared men do. That never occurred to Wilt. He's so gullible. I had to help him."

My mouth dropped open. Suddenly Wilt's gambling problem made sense. "Wilt is no stranger to Vegas, is he?"

"No," Aunt Pearl said in a small voice. "Wilt had to get the money somehow, and I figured there was no harm in helping him. Wilt and I were a team, but Manny and Bones both discovered our card counting system. Bones threatened to tell Manny, and I knew that Manny wouldn't hesitate to kill us both if we didn't stop."

"Well, why didn't you stop? That gave both of you a motive to kill Bones. Did you put that bullet in his forehead?" I already knew the answer, but I had to ask.

Aunt Pearl sobbed softly. "No, but Wilt did."

CHAPTER 36

"Wilt's a killer? I can't believe it." I stood and paced back and forth.

Aunt Pearl sighed. "Anybody can snap, Cen. Especially where family's involved."

"What do you mean by that? Who is Wilt's family?" My hand flew to my mouth. "Wilt is related to Bones?"

Aunt Pearl nodded. "Wilt is Bones' grandson. He even had a DNA test to prove it, but Bones still denied it. He claimed Wilt was an imposter, that Wilt had somehow doctored the test results."

"How can you be sure Wilt is telling the truth? Maybe he made it all up."

Aunt Pearl shook her head. "Wilt isn't the one who discovered the connection. I remember when Wilt was born and knew his family. Wilt was just a baby when he and his mother, Della, innocent bystanders, were caught in the crossfire of a gangland hit. Wilt's father died too, but he was part of the shootout.

"Wilt didn't die that day, but we didn't know it at the time. Della shielded him from the gunfire with her body, and that saved his life. But Carla only found that out many years later. It was a secret, known only to Bones and whoever had helped him cover it up. Long story short, Wilt lost both his parents that day.

"Bones felt so guilty about his daughter's death that he couldn't even bear to look at her son. Officially, Wilt's body was never found. Unofficially, he was placed in a foster home under another identity. Wilt was too young to know about his real parents, or that he had a grandfather nearby who had disowned him. Bones sent the foster home money every month but kept it top secret. Wilt grew up knowing nothing about his real identity."

"Then how…"

"Carla found out about the secret payments shortly after marrying Danny and wondered what they were for. She had an investigator look into the foster home. The payments went back decades, to around the time of the shootout that had killed Wilt's parents, and supposedly Wilt himself. She had always wondered why the little boy's body had never been found. Now it all made sense."

"How could she be sure it was him?"

"That birthmark on his forehead is unique. It still looked the same as it had when he was a baby," Aunt Pearl said. "You can imagine how all this went down when we reunited him with Bones."

I gasped. "Carla confronted him?"

"Of course she did. She wanted Danny to acknowledge his grandson. She abhorred the idea that Wilt had grown up in poverty as a government ward, when just a few miles away, his grandfather lived in the lap of luxury."

"And Bones—I mean, Danny—still wanted it covered up after all these years. He wanted to pretend that Wilt had never existed." Maybe Wilt would have been better off having never known that Danny "Bones" Battilana was his grandfather. It wasn't working out too well for him at the moment.

Aunt Pearl nodded. "Carla forced the issue with him, and he

finally admitted Wilt's existence. Of course that just made him look bad, and he didn't want the news getting out."

I frowned, realizing it also gave Wilt a strong motive to kill Bones. "Why did Carla wait decades to expose the truth?"

"She always felt guilty about it, and she was afraid of Bones. But as she got older, it bothered her more and more. She didn't want Wilt to go through life never knowing. It ate her up inside, knowing that she could make things right. In the end, her conscience won out."

Realization dawned on me. "That's why Bones killed Carla, isn't it? It wasn't to gain control of the Racatelli business. It was because he wanted Wilt's existence kept secret at all costs."

Aunt Pearl nodded. "Bones strangled Carla, then put her in the pool to make it look like an accident. He got away with it too, since he will never be charged." She glared at Christophe.

"He's dead, so in the end he got away with nothing," I pointed out.

"You give me enough proof, we can always reopen the case," Christophe said.

Aunt Pearl pointed to the autopsy report. She handed it to Christophe. "Like the report says, Carla was dead before she hit the water."

"There was no water in her lungs because she was already dead." I pointed to the bottom of the page. "Her death was ruled a homicide, yet the police called it an accident." I just hoped that what Aunt Pearl had provided was the real autopsy report and not something made up.

Christophe took the papers from Pearl. "I'll follow up myself with the medical examiner."

Aunt Pearl grew more and more uneasy as she talked. She kept glancing at her watch as a thin sheen of sweat covered her forehead. She was a definite flight risk and wouldn't incriminate herself without a little encouragement. I kept my hand on her back and motioned for her to sit down on the sofa. "Keep talking."

"I only know what Wilt told me," Aunt Pearl said. "Wilt wanted to confront his grandfather once Carla told him the truth. He was heartbroken when he learned that his own flesh and blood grandfather had abandoned him. Unfortunately, Wilt had a gambling problem, and it just got worse. Before he even had a chance to confront Danny, he had rung up a huge gambling debt."

"But you only met Wilt in Westwick Corners," I said. "You told me we were going to Las Vegas for Carla's funeral."

"How do you think I heard of Carla's funeral in the first place?" Aunt Pearl rose from the sofa and paced back and forth. "Wilt sought me out immediately after Carla died. She had secretly reunited with Wilt a few months ago."

"Reunited? I don't understand."

"Carla was Wilt's godmother. She was like a mother to Della, so she had been very attached to Della's baby. She was the one who broke the news to Wilt about his true identity." Aunt Pearl wiped a tear from her cheek. "Carla called me and asked if I would protect him if needed. Then she died suddenly. That's when Wilt came to me. He witnessed Carla's murder because he was staying right here in the suite."

"Why didn't you mention any of this to the police before?" Now I understood why Wilt preferred to stay in the RV rather than the suite.

"Bones always did whatever he wanted, and there were never any repercussions," Aunt Pearl said. "I didn't want to put Wilt in danger because Bones wouldn't knowingly leave any witnesses. Of course, none of that matters now."

"Maybe, but he's dead now, so he didn't exactly get away with murder."

"No, but poor Wilt's days are numbered, even with police protection."

"Wait a sec—if Carla died first, and Bones, her legal husband, died second, doesn't Wilt become the surviving heir, rather than Rocco?"

Aunt Pearl nodded slowly. "Now you see my problem? This isn't over by a long shot."

CHAPTER 37

Two uniformed police officers led a dejected and exhausted-looking Wilt into the suite. "You sure you want us to bring him here?"

Christophe nodded. "I want to check out a few things first. You guys stay in the foyer and watch the elevator. I don't want anyone coming in here, got it?"

The older of the two officers nodded and they stepped back out into the foyer, guns drawn.

Wilt held up his handcuffed wrists. "It was an accident. I just pointed the gun at Danny, but then he fought me for it. We wrestled and it went off. I never meant to kill him."

"No more talking till we get you a lawyer." Aunt Pearl made a slicing motion across her throat, before throwing her cell phone at me. "Cen, call one."

I caught my aunt's cell phone and scowled. "You could have let me borrow your phone earlier." She had kept it from me on purpose.

"It's not all about you, Cen." Aunt Pearl turned to Christophe. She glared at Christophe. "It was self defense. Any fool can see that."

Christophe ignored her. "Why'd you do it, Wilt? Why did you wait all these years?"

"I didn't wait. I had no idea I had any living relatives until Carla told me a few days ago. She felt it was my right to know that I was a Battilana, even if Danny denied it."

Aunt Pearl held up her hand. "Wilt—stop."

"No, I want to talk, lawyer or not. I want to clear things up." Wilt took a deep breath. "I was sleeping upstairs the day Carla died. I awoke to yelling and screaming coming from the patio. I recognized Carla's voice, and she was arguing with a man. The argument escalated so I ran outside to the patio. But it was too late. I couldn't save Carla."

Christophe scribbled furiously in his notebook, then fiddled with his phone. "Mind if I record this?"

Wilt shook his head. "I've got nothing to hide. By the time I got outside, Danny had his hands around Carla's neck. When he let go, she went limp. She wasn't breathing, but I tried CPR before Danny pulled me off."

"Poor Carla," Aunt Pearl said. "I told her not to, just to leave things be. But she insisted it was the right thing to do. That's the real reason Bones strangled her."

Suddenly it all made sense. Wilt's sudden appearance at the Westwick Corners Gas & Go. He had come to Aunt Pearl, Carla's closest friend, for help. Unfortunately for Wilt, Aunt Pearl didn't always think logically. Her crazy plan just made things worse, to the point that they had escalated almost out of control.

"What happened next, Wilt?" Tyler asked.

"The next few moments are a bit of a blur. Danny hit me over the head with a chair, and I blacked out. When I came to, he was dragging Carla into the pool. That's when I grabbed the gun from the desk over there." He pointed to the ornate French provincial desk a few feet away from the patio doors.

"I only grabbed it to scare him. I didn't even know whether the gun was loaded; I had no time to check. Danny came after me and wrestled me to the ground. The next thing I knew, the gun had gone off. For a second I thought it just shot into the air, but then Danny collapsed on top of me. I knew then that the bullet had hit him."

"That's when you called me," Aunt Pearl said. "It was self defense."

My eyes met Mom's and I saw she was thinking the same thing. Aunt Pearl was potentially an accessory to murder. She had almost certainly helped Wilt dispose of the body.

Strangely, Christophe didn't ask about that. Instead, he walked out to the foyer and said something to the uniformed men. Seconds later they departed in the elevator.

"Manny La Manna's been arrested for money laundering and racketeering," Christophe said. "Other charges are pending, but I'm not at liberty to say what those are right now."

"Where's Rocco? Is he okay?" I envisioned a Rocco-Manny standoff, and I wasn't sure that Rocco would come out unscathed.

Christophe nodded. "He's fine. He's been helping us for quite some time in our La Manna family investigation. Unlike Carla, he was never involved in any criminal activities. He never wanted to be a part of the Racatelli crime organization, but like it or not, he was born into it."

"Why isn't he here?"

"He will be, once he's finished being interviewed. It was his idea for you ladies to stay here. He was surprised when all of you showed up, and he was worried for your safety."

The intermingled crime families confused me enough, but the marriages baffled me even more. "But what about Carla's marriage to Manny? Won't he, as Carla's husband, inherit Carla's estate?"

"No," said Christophe. "Their marriage was real, but it was also null and void, since Carla was already married to Danny. Her fake marriage to Danny ended up being real after all."

Mom gasped. "She was a bigamist. Then who is Carla's heir? If it's still Bones—I mean Danny, then everything goes to Wilt."

Wilt waved his cuffed hands. "I don't want it."

"You won't get it. Bones can't inherit because he killed Carla. Therefore Wilt couldn't inherit from Bones. Once all the legal stuff is sorted out, Rocco will be the sole heir. Just like before," Aunt Pearl said.

"You're sure Rocco didn't—" The elevator bell sounded and my voice caught in my throat. Manny had been arrested, but maybe he had sent one of his henchmen for us.

Nobody else seemed concerned but me.

"Yes, I'm sure," said Christophe. "We had him under twenty-four-hour surveillance in the weeks before Carla's death, which continued up until this moment. Speaking of which, here he is."

Rocco strode into the suite, beaming. "I'm so relieved all this is finally over. I need a stiff drink."

Aunt Pearl tilted her head towards Christophe. "Chris, do the honors."

Mom rose from her seat and limped towards the kitchen. "Let me. Christophe shared his drink recipes with me and I'm anxious to experiment. Back in a flash."

"How about a margarita, Ruby?" Rocco smiled.

Mom limped to the kitchen and paused in the doorway. "Forget the margarita. I'm making you Christophe's special wine spritzer. You know, the one that incapacitates people."

Mom winked at me. "That drink is super handy in a pinch. I can already think of a few ways to use it."

CHAPTER 38

*A*unt Pearl, Mom, and I sat at neighboring slot machines. I was sandwiched in the middle and felt trapped. I was stuck with them, at least until Tyler returned from the police station. He had accompanied Christophe down to the station to provide a little more background on the events of the last few hours and, I assumed, say hello to some of his former colleagues.

I robotically pulled the handle down, hoping for that elusive three of a kind. We had been here for over an hour, and I had nothing to show for it. Aunt Pearl, on the other hand, seemed to be on a winning streak.

She leaned closer to me. "I used a spell on Manny to neutralize him." Aunt Pearl winked at me. "Just like I did on you and Rocco."

"I knew it! All those weird feelings I had for Rocco made no sense. And I'd hardly call that spell neutral."

"Okay, red hot." Aunt Pearl laughed.

"You manipulated me. How could you do such a thing?" Aside from being downright devious, it threatened to sabotage my developing relationship with Tyler. Of course, that was exactly what

Aunt Pearl wanted. The idea of me dating the sheriff had her knickers in a knot.

Or did it? I suddenly had doubts about Tyler and me. What if he wasn't really attracted to me? What if instead of his feelings, it was one of Aunt Pearl's spells?

How would I ever know what was real and what was contrived?

It would be the ultimate revenge, a twist of cruelty. "Did you do any other spells on me?"

"Like what?"

"Oh, I don't know. Any other love spells?"

"Relax, Cendrine. If you practiced your witchcraft at all, you would have immediately caught on to the spell. You could have counteracted it. It's really your own fault."

"Now Pearl…" Mom's protests fell on deaf ears.

Of course, I had caught onto the spell, but had decided to play dumb. With Aunt Pearl it was often better to play your cards close to your chest. She was completely unpredictable. But she was right about one thing.

I should respect and develop my natural talents. Maybe if I had the time, if I wasn't kept so busy extricating Aunt Pearl from multiple disasters and fiascos. But it was up to me to make time, and I intended to do exactly that.

If I tried hard enough, I could probably even put a spell on Aunt Pearl to keep her out of trouble. That spark of an idea energized me, and I could hardly wait to get back to my witchcraft. Only this time, I planned to do my lessons in secret, without Aunt Pearl as my instructor. I'd show her up.

I realized with a start that I was doing exactly what Aunt Pearl wanted me to do in the beginning. But rather than my aunt's imposed witchcraft lessons, I was doing it of my own free will.

"I don't get you, Pearl," Mom said. "You're already a millionaire. Why are you even playing the slots?"

"Heck, I could buy this place," Pearl said. "I'm richer than all of you combined."

I glared at her. "You don't need to rub it in our faces."

Aunt Pearl laughed. "I won't have it for long. Whatever's left after Wilt's legal bills will go to my favorite charity."

"Oh? What's that?" Mom asked.

"The Westwick Corners Revitalization Society."

"But we don't have a society." All we had was elbow grease. Aunt Pearl's constant complaints about tourist interlopers seemed contrary to the idea of sprucing things up to attract people. The idea that she would contribute to bringing visitors to Westwick Corners defied logic. I simply didn't believe her.

I felt eyes on me and turned around to face Rocco. The physical attraction I had felt earlier was gone, but it was replaced with something new. Instead of the dislike I had for the old Rocco, I now felt a genuine warmth. Age and distance had changed both of us, and now that the spell was gone I felt something I had never felt for him before.

Friendship.

"Who's up for a nice steak dinner?" Rocco motioned towards the street. "There's a nice little Italian restaurant nearby."

"Will there be gangsters?" Mom asked.

"Can't guarantee anything, but I certainly hope so." Rocco stared wistfully towards the bar. "I'm gonna miss this place, but not the gambling and crime that goes along with it."

Aunt Pearl squinted. "Oh no, look who's coming."

I met Tyler's gaze and smiled. "He can join us for dinner."

"Do you really have to invite him?" Aunt Pearl scowled. "I think I've lost my appetite."

I suddenly had the urge to try out the friendship spell I had secretly been practicing.

I snapped my fingers twice, then whispered the spell under my breath. "Let's go."

Aunt Pearl beamed as Tyler slipped his arm into hers. "What could be nicer than dinner with such a handsome escort?"

Tyler winked and I smiled back.

Aunt Pearl wasn't the only one with a trick up her sleeve.

CHAPTER 39

With Carla's murder solved, and Wilt behind bars for the murder of Danny "Bones" Battilana, there was no reason to stay in Las Vegas any longer.

Aunt Pearl was unlikely to cause much more trouble, but I couldn't rest until I knew she was safely out of town. I insisted that Aunt Pearl and Mom book commercial airline tickets back home. Once that was done, we headed straight for the airport.

Tyler walked ahead of us through the bustling Las Vegas airport, loaded down with Mom and Aunt Pearl's luggage on each arm. Mom clutched a folder full of Christophe's drink recipes, while Aunt Pearl carried a small bag. I had no idea what it contained, but I decided not to ask. Sometimes it was better not to know, especially when it concerned my aunt. She had to pass through security, so I wasn't too worried.

I widened the gap until we were out of earshot in the noisy airport. "Remember, no witchcraft on the plane. You don't want to freak out the crew or passengers. There could even be undercover Air Marshals."

"Don't use your scare tactics on me, missy." Aunt Pearl's jovial mood had vanished. "I've already resigned myself to captivity in that airborne sardine can. You don't have to rub it in."

In a weird way, it felt good to see Aunt Pearl back to her normal cranky self.

"Don't worry, Cen. We'll act normal." Mom squeezed my hand.

"You really don't have to follow us all the way to security. We're perfectly capable of taking care of ourselves," Aunt Pearl protested.

"Maybe a little too capable," I said. "I want to see you get on the plane." I was confident that my aunt wouldn't pull any tricks once she was onboard. But until she passed through the security gate, she was a flight risk, so to speak. I had no illusions about that.

"I don't see why we can't use a little magic," Aunt Pearl protested. "Ruby and I could have teleported back to Westwick Corners faster than it took to drive here."

"No more witchcraft, Aunt Pearl. At least not until you're safely back in Westwick Corners." I had arranged for Aunt Amber to meet them at the Shady Creek airport and drive them back to Westwick Corners.

Aunt Amber also happened to be a high-ranking WICCA official, so she had her own reasons for ensuring Aunt Pearl behaved. Whatever punishments WICCA handed out would likely be minimal, but at least Aunt Pearl had to answer to someone. The last thing she would risk losing was her license to practice witchcraft.

Somebody from the *Shady Creek Tattler* would almost certainly be waiting for Aunt Pearl and Mom's arrival, and that was one story I wanted to end well. "Don't do anything foolish that will hurt our quiet existence in Westwick Corners."

While she could technically teleport herself once away from my sight and on the plane, I counted on Mom to talk her out of it. People simply didn't disappear on commercial flights, and the last thing we needed was an airline incident attracting international attention. Since Aunt Pearl was already in hot water over her card counting scheme, I was fairly certain she wouldn't do anything foolish.

We stopped a few feet from the security gate.

"You're lucky that Wilt made a full confession, or you might not even be going back. You could be locked up in a cell like him." I glanced at Mom. "Keep an eye on her, and I'll see you in a few days."

"I think I need a vacation from my vacation." Mom laughed.

I was still unclear on exactly how much Aunt Pearl had won in the lottery. Apparently though, it was enough to hire a top-notch criminal defense lawyer for Wilt and cover his bail. Wilt planned to attend a gambling rehab program while he was awaiting trial. He was in good hands.

WE STOOD at the security check-in and said our goodbyes before Mom and Aunt Pearl passed through the security gate.

I turned to Tyler and kissed him on the cheek. "I can't believe you came all the way to Las Vegas. How did you know I'd need your help?"

"Just a hunch. I had a feeling you were in over your head." He pulled me towards him and pressed his lips to mine.

I wasn't sure if he was referring to the Racatellis or Aunt Pearl, but I didn't need an answer. I had other things on my mind.

We watched Mom and Aunt Pearl's flight take off and then headed back to the airport parking lot where the RV was parked. We planned to drive it back to the RV dealer in Shady Creek where Aunt Pearl had gotten it.

It turned out that the RV was real after all. Aunt Pearl hadn't conjured it up. She had taken it for a test drive and simply never returned it. She had made it disappear once simply to mislead me. It was the only thing about my aunt that was predictable; she would go out of her way to mislead me anytime she could. Outsmarting me was like a form of entertainment for her.

Everything else was true. Aunt Pearl really had won the lottery, and Wilt really was Danny "Bones" Battilana's grandson.

CHAPTER 40

The sun peeked through the low clouds as we drove north on the Interstate. We had passed through sun, rain, and, finally, a thunderstorm that had threatened to delay us at the mountains dividing Nevada and northern California. We crested the pass just as the sky brightened before us.

I glanced at Tyler in the RV driver's seat. It was strangely comforting to be in the middle of a storm with him, and strangely romantic in our refuge on wheels.

Manny's assets were seized, and he remained in jail without bail.

Rocco had decided to sell the hotel and distance himself from "the family." An anonymous investor had already made Rocco a generous offer (with encouragement from Aunt Pearl, of course) that allowed Rocco a gracious—and safe—exit.

Mom, Aunt Pearl, and a little magic would ensure Rocco's seamless transition to his new life. I wasn't sure exactly what it was, but that didn't matter.

"Oh, I almost forgot." Tyler reached behind the seat and handed me my purse. "I found it on the front seat when I had your car towed back home from the gas station."

I rummaged inside and pulled out my cell phone. I unlocked my phone, relieved that the battery was still good. I checked my voicemail. "It seems that word has already gotten out. *The Shady Creek Tattler* wants my story. In fact, they want to hire me on the spot."

Tyler smiled. "Are you going to take it?"

I shrugged. "I don't know. Maybe I'll sleep on it." I would have taken the job under any terms a few days ago. But with this latest adventure I realized that from now on, things would be on my own terms.

I suddenly realized that witchcraft gave me an advantage over other journalists. I could get stories other people couldn't, just by using my natural talents. Because that's what they were: perfectly natural. I just had to harness the power of something that was already mine.

"Let's go home." I smiled at Tyler as I scanned the radio for something upbeat.

"First things first," Tyler said. "Aren't we forgetting something?"

I raced through my mental checklist. Luggage, gas in the tank, and Mom and Aunt Pearl safely delivered to the airport.

Check.

I shook my head. "Nope. I think we've got everything covered."

"Our date?" Tyler grinned. "I traveled hundreds of miles to see you, yet we still haven't had our date."

I glanced at Tyler and smiled. I had gone from obsessing over our date, to barely thinking of it, now that Tyler was with me. Part of that was due to the enormity of the events unfolding, but the real reason was that just being together was all I needed. It felt like a date already. I didn't need a fancy dinner or night out, just the man beside me.

I still felt bad, though.

"I'm really sorry about our date, Tyler. I never expected the kidnapping, Las Vegas, and everything." Aunt Pearl had a knack for always throwing a wrench into my plans. "I'll make it up to you, I promise."

"No, don't apologize. It's not your fault. Besides, I have an idea." He took the next highway exit, then turned right at a four-way stop a quarter mile later.

"Where on earth are we going?" There were no nearby towns, but the sole road sign advertised gas a quarter-mile away. There was only one way to Westwick Corners, and this wasn't it. This was one kidnapping I wasn't about to protest. "Better safe than sorry. Bad things happen when I run out of gas."

Tyler smiled. "It's not just gas we need. You'll see."

We slowed as the pavement turned to dirt and potholes. The narrow road wound around a steep hillside, with barely enough room for a car to pass in the opposite direction. Not that we saw much traffic. I wondered about the viability of a gas station in the middle of nowhere.

A few minutes later we arrived at the gas station. Nine Mile Gap was a tiny hamlet in the middle of nowhere. It was already mid-morning, but there was no sign of life anywhere, including the advertised gas station, a tiny sheet metal building with a single rusted pump. It was deader than dead.

"This place doesn't look nine miles to anywhere." I stared at the dust and grease covered windows as we pulled up to the gas island.

"Not anymore. This is where I grew up," Tyler said. "Used to be like Westwick Corners back then. Now it's more of a ghost town."

"Even the gas station is closed." The sole gas pump was rusted, with weeds entwining the nozzle. The old-style numbers that turned as the gas pumped were frozen in time at a price of twenty cents a gallon. I felt bad for Tyler.

The passage of time was rarely kind to memories. You could never go back in time without disappointment. Things were rarely the same as you remembered them.

"That's okay. We're not here for the gas." Tyler parked the RV at the far end of the lot and shut off the engine. "Our date starts now."

He hopped out of the driver's seat, walked around the RV, and opened my passenger door. "I know a nice little restaurant around here. It's a well-kept secret, very exclusive."

I stepped down from the RV, taking his outstretched hand.

We walked around the side of the gas station past an old three-storey brick building. We turned the corner and emerged onto a cobblestone street.

My mouth dropped open in amazement. We stood at the edge of Main Street in a completely restored 1950s era ghost town. Everything was spotless and freshly painted, yet there wasn't a soul around. It was as if time had come to a standstill in a bygone era.

"It was a company town, back in the day. Then the mine closed and it was all but forgotten."

I wondered what secrets this town held behind the neat façade.

We walked slowly down the street, my hand in his. "This reminds me of Westwick Corners, except quieter." I would never have thought that was possible, yet it was.

Tyler grinned. "I thought you'd like it. Now let's go. I've been looking forward to our date for ages."

I followed Tyler into a pretty little café with flower boxes overflowing with lavender and nasturtiums. The restaurant appeared to be the only place open for business. The floorboards squeaked beneath my feet as I stepped through the door into the dimly lit interior.

An attractive woman in her late forties emerged from the back to greet us and motioned us towards the side of the restaurant to a window booth. A ceiling fan hummed overhead, creating a refreshing breeze. I followed the woman to a booth overlooking a burbling creek surrounded by lush greenery. It was like we were in another world. "Here okay?" The hostess winked at Tyler, who nodded.

"It's beautiful." I sighed as I slid into the booth seat.

The woman smiled at me as she handed us menus. Tyler ordered Cokes for both of us.

I waited until our hostess was halfway to the kitchen before I looked up from my menu. "I hope you're not too disappointed about the French restaurant and all. I'll make it up to you somehow."

Tyler grinned. "It really doesn't matter where we go. In fact, this might be even better."

I scrunched up my nose. "I know what you mean. Fancy restaurants usually have tiny portions. Right now I could eat a horse."

Tyler laughed. "That's not what I meant."

"What then?" Suddenly it dawned on me. "The hostess recognized you right away. You've been back to this restaurant recently."

"Plenty of times, Cen."

All of a sudden I felt weird. "What is it? You two know each other, don't you?"

"I wondered when you'd notice. It's not just that this is my hometown, Cen. That woman is my mom."

"Your mom?" My mouth dropped open and all of a sudden I felt self-conscious as I looked down at my dusty clothing. I re-tied my messy ponytail. "You never said you came from a small town."

He laughed. "You never asked."

"But I just assumed that since you worked in Las Vegas, that you were from there."

"Pretty much everyone there comes from somewhere else, Cen. Since I know your family already, I thought you might as well meet mine."

Now it was my turn to laugh. "No wonder you like Westwick Corners. It's practically bustling compared to here. But it's got to be hard to make a living here. How does your mom do it?"

"She doesn't exactly. She has another line of business."

Before I had a chance to ask more, Tyler's mom appeared with our Cokes. In hindsight the resemblance was obvious. Tyler's mom had the same warm brown eyes and welcoming smile as her son.

"Mom, meet Cen. Cen, this is my mom, Vivica."

"Here you go, dear." She smiled at me as she placed my glass down, then Tyler's. "I heard about the trouble in Vegas. I'm glad Ty helped you out."

"Cen didn't need my help, Mom. She took care of things just fine."

I blushed. "It was nothing, really. Just some family business." Whether I liked it or not, Aunt Pearl's troubles were mine too. Whatever Aunt Pearl's faults, she was loyal to those she cared about, and she would help me too.

"I heard you handled yourself pretty well." Vivica Gates smiled. "Considering you were sort of thrown into the middle of things."

I wondered exactly what and how much Tyler had told his mom. In the end, it didn't really matter. What was done was done. People could draw their own conclusions.

I changed the subject. "Nine Mile Gap seems awfully quiet."

Vivica sighed. "The town has seen better days, for sure. Only a few of us still live here now."

"I'm sorry to hear that," I said. "My town is the same way. Everyone is moving away to bigger places."

Vivica nodded. "Tyler told me all about your Inn and your plans to resurrect the town."

"You could do that too," I said. "You just need a way to market the town to tourists."

"Oh, don't get me wrong. I quite like the solitude. I can do my magic in peace. It's nice to not have to hide your talents."

Tyler smiled at me. "You two have a lot in common."

"You're a-uh…" I couldn't quite say it.

"A witch." Vivica finished my sentence. "Yes. That I am."

My mouth dropped open. No wonder Tyler handled Aunt Pearl's antics so well. Suddenly everything made sense. "This is your big secret, isn't it? The one that Aunt Pearl's always going on about." I had always assumed it was something bad, a dark spot in Tyler's past.

His brown eyes twinkled in amusement. "You think there are no other witches around?"

"You know about us."

"Of course I know. I can spot a witch a mile away."

"You know about me?"

Tyler nodded. "Though I haven't seen any evidence of it. Either you're very good, or completely out of practice."

I grinned. "I've been told that I'm both."

"You probably take after Pearl that way. Am I right?"

"Yes." For the first time ever, I was really proud to be a witch. And Aunt Pearl's niece to boot. "You're okay with all my quirks?"

"Of course, though I'd hardly call witchcraft a quirk, Cen." Tyler placed his hand on mine. "I'd accept you for who you are no matter what. That's just what makes you so special. The witchcraft is a bonus."

Tyler's reaction was a refreshing change from my last boyfriend, who saw my supernatural talents as embarrassing and potentially career-ending.

"It's kind of nice to see Tyler with a girl somewhat like his mother." Vivica laughed. "I don't have to pretend I'm normal either. I can just be myself." She turned and headed into the kitchen with our orders.

"I had no idea you were, um..." I was suddenly at a loss for words.

"A son of a witch?" Tyler grinned as he squeezed my hand.

I burst out laughing. "Exactly the words I was looking for."

For the first time in a long time, I felt good about every aspect of myself. I was comfortable in my own skin. I didn't have to hide my talents or pretend I was someone else. I could just be me.

Here I was, a thousand miles away from Westwick Corners in a town I had never been in before. And yet, I was completely at home.

Love Rags to Witches? Get the next in the series, Witch and Famous

www.colleencross.com

AFTERWORD

If you enjoyed *Rags to Witches,* please recommend it to your friends and leave a short review. Feedback helps me determine which series to continue to write, and informs other readers too. Just a sentence or two is fine.

Rags to Witches is the second book in the *Westwick Witches Cozy Mysteries* series and I have many more books planned. As long as readers like you enjoy my stories, I will continue to write them.

Want to be the first to know of new releases? Sign up for notifications at www.colleencross.com

I have several other mystery and thriller series that you might enjoy. Check out the links on the next page.

Thank you so much for reading!

Colleen Cross

ABOUT THE AUTHOR

Mystery and crime thriller author Colleen Cross writes exciting, intelligent thrillers and engrossing mysteries that grip you from the very first page. She took her very own "Exit Strategy" from the corporate world into the book world several years ago to indulge her bookworm wannabe writer self.

Colleen Cross is a retired CPA and CFO who lives with her family on Canada's West Coast. When not writing she loves to run, hike, and explore the coast and mountains with her rescue dog, Jaeger, who reminds her daily that life's too short to not follow your dreams--or a squirrel or two.

Her thriller and mystery books have been translated into multiple languages with more to come. Find them in Dutch, French, German, Italian, Portuguese, Spanish and other languages using search term Colleen Cross

Visit her website at www.colleencross.com and sign up for new release notifications and exclusive subscriber-only offers at http:// eepurl.com/bkYx01 or click the QR code below:

Get the latest on Colleen's books here:
www.colleencross.com

ALSO BY COLLEEN CROSS

Westwick Witches Cozy Mysteries

Witch You Well

Rags to Witches

Witch and Famous

Christmas Witch List

Witching Hour Dead

Witching for Love on Valentines Day

Katerina Carter Fraud Legal Thrillers

Exit Strategy

Game Theory

Blowout

Greenwash

Red Handed

Blue Moon

Nonfiction

Anatomy of a Ponzi Scheme